FATAL CHOCOLATE OBSESSION

Sally Berneathy

Chapter One

Closing time on Monday afternoon always feels like a major accomplishment. For some reason, that day seems longer than any other.

I flipped the sign on the front door of Death by Chocolate to *Closed* and started to lock up. However, before I turned the key, I noticed a red rose stuck in the door.

I would have liked to think Trent, my special cop, happened by and left it, but that wasn't his style. He's more likely to show up with a bag of burgers and rings than flowers.

I opened the door and let the rose fall to the sidewalk then picked it up. This was more Rickhead's style, my annoying ex. Last I heard, his latest bimbo, Ginger, was sharing my former house with my former husband, but Rick goes through women like I go through chocolate. I sincerely hoped the rose wasn't a sign he was going to renew his salesman tactics on me. He does that occasionally when he's between girlfriends.

Probably somebody dropped it on the walk in front of my shop then somebody else picked it up and stuck it in the door. It did have a short stem and looked as if it could have been lying on the street and kicked around for a while. Poor rose. I took it inside, locked the door behind me, and put it in a paper cup of water.

Paula came in from the kitchen with a broom. She stopped and scowled at the rose sitting on the counter. "Where did you get that?"

"Front door." I gathered the remaining dirty dishes from a couple of tables.

"Who put it there?"

"How would I know? Do you want me to have Fred dust it for fingerprints?"

"You don't know who left it there but you brought it inside?" She walked across the room, giving the flower a wide berth but watching it carefully as if it might suddenly explode, showering the entire restaurant with aphids or anthrax.

She leaned the broom against the wall and began stacking chairs on tables. "You have no idea where that flower's been, and it's certainly a little odd to find it stuck in the door." She began sweeping vigorously...viciously, actually. "Speaking of odd, I saw your friend Bob lurking in the alley. Probably waiting for you to take him some more food."

Paula tends to be cynical sometimes. Most times, actually. But she's entitled after her abusive ex-husband hunted her down and tried to take her son as well as kill her best friend, namely me. She has to be cynical and suspicious to protect her three year old

2

son. I don't have to. I only have a cat, and he's pretty self-sufficient. Besides, I'm dating a cop, and he's cynical and suspicious enough for both of us.

I set more chairs on more tables. "Bob's not lurking," I said in response to her accusation. "He's just…well, visiting."

"He's a homeless bum."

"He's out of work."

"For five years."

I thrust my chin forward. "Because his wife died and he lost his company."

Paula didn't reply. She really does have a soft heart hidden somewhere behind all that cynicism. She just tries very hard not to let anybody except her son know about it.

I grabbed a bag and tossed in a couple of chicken sandwiches along with three chocolate chip cookies and a chocolate nut cupcake.

Paula raised an eyebrow.

"Leftovers. You know any food we don't take home and eat tonight will just get thrown away. Bob might as well eat it." I checked to be sure she had returned to her sweeping then added a can of Coke and a bottle of water. He needed liquids. It was the middle of September and still quite warm outside.

Paula didn't look up. "Leftover Coke and water?" Woman has eyes in the top of her head.

"I'll be right back."

I'd noticed Bob a few weeks ago. When I went out to dump the leftovers one evening, he was going through the trash bin, looking for food. I stopped and turned to run that first time. He was a big man with thick dark hair and beard. He hadn't shaved or had a hair cut in a very long time and he looked quite fierce. But before I could get back inside, he stepped away from the dumpster and mumbled an apology.

Instead of throwing my food in the trash bin, I handed it directly to him. He hesitated then accepted the bag and thanked me profusely.

For the next few days I made sure to leave a bag of leftovers for him to find. At first he waited down the alley and only approached when he thought I was back inside. Before long we became buddies and, in response to my nosy questions, he told me his story. His wife died of cancer five years ago after a long illness. With all the expenses and his depression over his wife's death, he lost his small construction business…then his house…then his dignity.

Bob had potential. He just needed a little encouragement to get his life back on track. I consider myself good at that sort of thing. Paula says I'm bossy. I say, whatever works. It had only been a few weeks and Bob was already showing signs of coming around, talking about possibilities of getting a job and reclaiming his life.

I clutched my bag of goodies and walked out the back door into the alley. Bob leaned against the wall with his back toward me, but when I closed the door, he stood straight and faced me.

I stopped and blinked in surprise. "You shaved!"

He grinned, the expression quite pleasant now that I could see his face. "And I cut my hair."

I moved closer and checked him out. "So you did!" He'd even changed the shabby clothes he usually wore for a clean, hole-free pair of blue jeans and a faded blue striped shirt. "You look..." I stopped myself from saying *civilized* or something equally insulting. "Nice. You look very nice."

The face I was seeing for the first time turned bright pink with pleasure. "I got a job."

"A job? Oh, Bob, that's wonderful! Tell me all about it."

He shrugged but I could tell from his smile and the gleam in his eyes that he was bursting with pride. "It's no big deal. I talked to an old friend, somebody I used to know when I was in the construction business. He's going to take me on as assistant superintendent."

"That's fantastic!" I rushed forward and gave him an impulsive hug.

He grunted and I realized I'd whacked him with the bag containing the food and drinks.

I stepped back and offered him the sack which by that time contained smashed sandwiches and crumbled cookies.

The flush on his face deepened as he accepted the food. Maybe he'd been blushing every time I saw him and I couldn't tell because of the beard.

"It's no big deal," he repeated. "I'll basically be a go-fer to start with, but Nick knows what I can do. He said when I prove myself, he'll put me in charge of a small job and we can go from there."

"It *is* a big deal! I'm so proud of you!"

"Lindsay, I'm going to pay you back for this." He lifted the bag. "For all of it. I couldn't have done this without your help."

It was my turn to blush, and, being a redhead, I do a really good job of it. "I just gave you what I was going to dispose of anyway."

He laughed softly. To think I'd actually been afraid of this gentle man the first time I saw him. Appearances can be deceiving. "You fed me and you pushed me into shaping up."

I started to protest, but I had encouraged him. Actually, once I realized he had marketable skills, I suppose I sort of pushed him. Maybe I was even a little bossy, as Paula accused. But it was for his own good.

"It's okay," he said. "You were right. I have to quit feeling sorry for myself and get up and fight. It's what Linda would want. When she died, I wanted to die with her, but I didn't. So I guess I have to live. I don't expect to have the wonderful life I had before, but I'm going to do the best I can to be sure I don't have to take handouts ever again. Thank you."

I shrugged. "It's the chocolate. It gives you energy and will power."

He laughed. "Your chocolate desserts turn homeless bums into Supermen."

"That sounds right." I don't believe in false modesty.

He left and I went inside to tell Paula the good news.

❧❧

I swear I was not speeding at the time of the accident. I know how unlikely that sounds, but I was almost home and in no hurry. The afternoon was pleasant and warm. Brilliant yellows and reds blazed among the green in the tapestry of trees. I was driving with my sunroof open, listening to country music, enjoying the day, thinking about Bob and how he was turning his life around when…*bam!*

If I'd been speeding, I might have got away from the car before it hit me, which just goes to show, speeding is not necessarily a bad thing. It certainly should not be considered a crime, punishable by tickets and points on my insurance and fees to lawyers and lectures from Trent.

But as soon as I felt that lurch and heard that crunching noise, I knew my record with those stupid speeding tickets would come back to haunt me.

I sighed, turned off the engine and got out.

The attacking car was an older model beige sedan that appeared to have taken the brunt of the accident. However, it had been in better shape to start with so the dent was more obvious. My elderly but still fast Celica already had a few dents and scrapes, and the Kansas City sun had faded its once brilliant red color to a softer hue, a completely inappropriate hue. A car like mine should be brightly colored.

A man wearing faded blue jeans and a work shirt got out of the car behind me. I straightened, readying my defenses as I walked toward him.

"I'm so sorry," he said.

That was a good beginning.

We met at the place our cars met and looked down.

He lifted his gaze to mine. Sad puppy dog eyes. "It's all my fault."

Beautiful words.

"It doesn't look like there's much damage." If he was going to take the blame and his car had more damage than mine, maybe we could walk away from this with my insurance company none the wiser.

The young man with puppy dog eyes pointed to a dent in the back of my car where his bumper was higher than mine. "I did that. I'll fix it for you."

This was the part where we had to exchange insurance information. "Really, it's not that bad. I'm going to have my car repainted soon, and one more dent won't make much difference."

He studied me closely, squinting against the afternoon sun. "You don't remember me, do you, Lindsay?"

I focused my attention on him rather than on the damaged cars and how this was going to affect my already precarious insurance situation. He was a big guy, but not Sumo wrestler big. More like an overgrown teddy bear. He had brown hair, brown eyes, no scars or tattoos…the kind of guy you could watch rob a bank then be unable to identify in a line-up. But the puppy dog eyes rang a faint, distant bell.

"Of course I remember you!" I didn't, but since he wasn't my neighbor and he wasn't the guy I was dating, he had to either be one of the cops who loved to write speeding tickets for me or a customer at Death by Chocolate. He didn't act like a cop. "You love my chocolate chip cookies!" Another educated guess. Everybody loves my chocolate chip cookies.

A wide smile spread across his face and sparkled in his eyes. "Today I had your chocolate nut cupcake."

I returned his smile. "Of course! You come in for lunch, and you always sit at the counter." I was still guessing but feeling more confident. He looked vaguely familiar.

He beamed and held out a large hand. "I'm Brandon Mathis."

Despite his meek demeanor, his handshake was surprisingly firm and strong.

"I feel really bad about this," he said. "To tell you the truth, I saw the red hair and thought that might be you. I guess I was paying too much attention to you and not enough to my driving."

I resisted the urge to release a deep sigh of relief. The worst thing that would come out of this encounter would be another dent in my already dented car. My insurance company and my cop boyfriend need never know. Not that the accident was my fault. Brandon had graciously accepted all responsibility. But somehow insurance companies and cops always seem to place some of the blame on me just because I don't agree with those arbitrary speed limits.

"Don't worry about it," I said. "Seriously, I'm planning to get a new paint job in the near future. When you come in tomorrow, I'll give you a chocolate chip cookie on the house."

He shook his head. "No, that's not right. I hit your car and you give me a cookie?" He reached into the pocket of his faded jeans and produced a slightly crumpled business card. "I can take care of this. I fix cars. My dad and I own a repair shop."

I accepted the card and read the black print on a white background. *Mathis Paint and Body Shop.* The address wasn't far from Death by Chocolate.

This guy looked too crisp and clean to work on cars. After spending the day in a hot kitchen, I had chocolate in my hair and on my T-shirt, but Brandon had no grease or paint on his clothing. Maybe he had already changed clothes after work.

He walked past me and studied my car more closely. "This is almost a classic. They don't make these anymore."

"I know. That's why I'm having mine repainted. Restored." That word took my car from old to classic.

"The last one came out in 2006."

"Two thousand five," I corrected.

"Two thousand five for the US, but they had a 2006 model in Japan only."

The man knew his Celicas.

He peeked in my open window. "Five on the floor. Good choice. More power than with the automatic."

It was my turn to beam. I do enjoy having my chocolate creations and my Celica complimented.

"If you're going to have this car repainted anyway, I'd love to have the chance to do it. I'll make you a deal. Fifty percent off since I caused part of the damage, and a loaner car while the work's being done." He slid a hand along the spoiler, his touch caressing. "It won't be as much fun to drive as this one, but it'll get you around until I finish."

That did sound like a deal. I was ready to follow him to his repair shop, drop off my car and get on with it, but I knew I'd catch a load of grief from cynical Paula, distrusting Detective Adam Trent, and my neighbor, OCD Fred, if I didn't check this guy out first. Not that he needed checking out. If he was a regular customer and loved my chocolate, what else did I need to know? Those attributes spoke volumes for his character.

I held up his card. "That sounds great. I'll check my schedule and get back to you."

He grasped my other hand and held it with both of his. "Thank you, Lindsay, for letting me take care of this and not going through the insurance companies and all that mess."

No wonder he was so eager to fix my car. He probably had a bunch of speeding tickets and an evil insurance company too. I'd been so relieved about the whole situation I hadn't even thought of his view of things. So we'd both be getting something out of this. Surely even Paula couldn't question the legitimacy of such a deal.

A warm glow surrounded me as I continued home. Bob had a job and I was going to get my car painted by a fan of my chocolate desserts. A great start to the week.

I pulled my Celica into the garage that listed slightly to one side and started across the yard to my front porch. The lawn was freshly mown.

Yard work was not on my priority list, but it was on Fred's. My neighbor has a priority list about fifty pages long. In fact, I can't think of anything in his life that isn't on his priority list. And at that moment my lawn was exactly the same height as his. He could have mowed both lawns while I was at work or his invisible but efficient elves could have done it or he could have waved his magic wand and shortened all the grass blades to exactly three inches. In any event, I was certain he had a hand in it.

Whenever my lawn mysteriously looks better, I take Fred extra chocolate. However, this time some of my clover, wild violets and dandelions looked terminally ill. I don't like having chemicals in my yard nor do I like killing off those pretty flowers. Who made the decision we could only have grass in our yards? Probably the same people who set up those stupid speed limits.

I marched past my house, straight to Fred's front door, and pressed the doorbell repeatedly. When no one answered, I pounded on the immaculate white frame then rattled the screen door. "Fred!"

"Yes, Lindsay?"

I whirled at the sound of his voice. He was standing behind me, tall and lanky with immaculate white hair and black-framed glasses, unruffled as always. "How did you get back there?" I demanded. "Have you got a trap door in your front porch or something?"

He scowled. "Sometimes I worry about you. I crossed the street from Sophie's house and walked up the steps while you were trying to beat down my door."

Ever since last month when Sophie Fleming moved into the house across the street, I'd suspected she and Fred had a thing going. I had no objection to the relationship. In fact, I approved of it. I just needed to know about it.

Although at four o'clock in the afternoon his presence at her house wasn't really indicative of much of anything, I had to ask. "So, how's Sophie?"

Fred moved around me and opened his door then held it for me to enter. "She's fine. Nothing's changed since you talked to her yesterday."

"I know, but this is early for her to be home. She's usually still decorating the homes of the rich and famous at this time of the day."

"She needed some help with financial planning so I offered my services."

I frowned. "Financial planning? What do you know about financial planning? You're a day trader."

He rolled his eyes. "Day trading is so yesterday. Do you want to come in or not?"

"No, I haven't been home to let Henry out yet."

"Then why were you standing on my front porch, banging on my door?"

"Oh, that, well…" I waved my arm toward my yard. "Thank you for mowing my lawn. Did you put that chemical stuff on it?"

"What makes you think I mowed your lawn? I'm making marinara sauce tonight. Would you like to come over for spaghetti?"

"Homemade garlic toast?"

He gave me a *duh* expression. "Of course."

So much for delivering an excoriating lecture about chemicals in the ground water and the importance of all-natural lawns. "I don't have any leftovers today, but I'll whip up something for dessert. Cookies? Brownies?"

"Brownies. See you in a couple of hours." He started through the door.

"Are you going to invite Sophie?" I called after him.

"She's putting together a proposal for a new client tonight."

Aha! He'd already asked her! Did he plan to have us both over, or was I second choice? Not that it mattered. Fred was sometimes my second choice if Trent couldn't come over. So...did that mean Sophie occupied the same place in Fred's life that Trent occupied in mine?

Actually, it did matter. If she wasn't a romantic interest, did that mean she'd taken my place as his best friend?

I peered closely at him, trying to read his thoughts.

He closed the door.

With my ego issues unresolved, I went home to feed my cat and let him out to roam the neighborhood. Shortly after he moved in, he informed me he was an indoor/outdoor cat. He weighs twenty-three pounds and has half inch claws. I accepted his choice. He doesn't go far and always returns home, sometimes with a present for me. We won't discuss his choice of presents. It's the thought that counts.

☙❧

I spent a pleasant evening eating Fred's delicious spaghetti, drinking red wine from crystal glasses and trying unsuccessfully to pry information out of him about his relationship with Sophie, his occupation, where he learned karate kicks and how to scan for listening devices—all the usual stuff.

In some ways Fred is like Henry. Henry appeared out of nowhere one day and took up residence in my house. I have no idea where he lived or what he did before he came to live with me, and he's not telling. Not that Fred took up residence in my house, but he won't tell me anything about his life before I became his neighbor.

Fred and Henry even have the same white hair and blue eyes, except Henry has gold markings and Fred doesn't shed. They pretend to have a haughty disdain for each other, but they have more in common than either wants to admit.

I gave Brandon's business card to Fred so he could check out the business before I entrusted my car to them.

At ten o'clock I thanked Fred for a wonderful meal, he thanked me for a wonderful dessert, and I headed home. No worries about having a couple of glasses of wine when I could always crawl to my house.

Henry met me on my front porch. I was relieved to see he had no gift for me.

"Have a good evening?" I asked.

He rubbed against my leg and purred. I took that to be an affirmative answer.

"Ready for a little catnip?"

He purred louder.

I unlocked my door and we went inside.

15

Henry likes his catnip straight, on a plate where he can snort it, lick it and rub his face in it. He's an addict. I have to keep the bag under lock and key. Well, I keep it in a drawer high enough he can't open it. At least, he hasn't been able to open it yet.

I grabbed a cookie and we headed upstairs to bed. There's nobody around to hide the cookies, so I get to indulge my addiction.

Henry settled at the foot of my bed and I slipped on my old, faded, worn, comfortable night shirt.

The doorbell rang.

I looked at my watch cat. He goes all jungle cat when someone he doesn't like is at the door. Tonight he seemed unperturbed. I wasn't sure if that meant my late-night caller was harmless or my watch cat was stoned.

I slipped on my jeans and went downstairs then flipped on the porch light and looked through the peephole. Trent stood on my front porch. That was a pleasant surprise. We don't usually get together except on weekends, but occasionally, when his work schedule allows, he drops by unexpectedly.

I flung the door wide. "Did you come over to play cops and robbers?" I asked suggestively.

Then I noticed he was not alone. His partner, Gerald Lawson, stood stolidly beside him. Oops.

Trent has brown eyes with traces of green that become brighter when he's happy. Even in the dimness of my porch light I could see that his eyes were dark brown without a hint of spring. He wasn't smiling or even blushing at my comment. We were probably not going to play cops and robbers. At least, not the fun version.

"Lindsay, we need to talk to you," he said.

Lawson, better known as Granite Man, looked grim and said nothing. He does that quite well.

My heart clenched into a tight little knot. I was pretty sure this wasn't a social call. Cops at my door in the middle of the night could only mean bad news.

My mind raced through a list of the people I loved, the people who could have been hurt...or worse. It couldn't be Fred. I'd just left him and besides, he's invulnerable. Henry was upstairs asleep. That left my mother, father, Paula, Zach, Sophie...

"Who?" One word was the most I could force through my lips.

"Do you know a man named Robert Markham?"

Not bad news about somebody I loved. My heart unclenched and I released the breath I'd been holding. "No."

"He got a to-go order from your place today. Two chicken sandwiches, several cookies, a cupcake, a can of Coke and a bottle of water."

I started to shake my head then frowned. That order sounded familiar. Robert Markham? Bob? The man who was trying to put his life back together? The man who got a haircut and a shave and a new job? I couldn't believe he'd regressed and done something so stupid the cops were after him.

"Why are you asking?"

Lawson remained grim and silent.

Trent shifted from one foot to the other and cleared his throat. "He was murdered in the alley behind Death by Chocolate."

Chapter Two

I swallowed hard and lifted a hand to my throat. "No, that can't be."

Trent's expression softened. "So you did know this guy?"

"Yes, I knew him."

"Good. We can't find a home address, next of kin, place of employment...nothing. The only ID he had on him was an expired driver's license with an address he doesn't live at. Any information you can give us will be helpful."

I sighed. "Come in and have a seat. I'll make some hot chocolate."

"Do you have coffee?" Lawson asked.

"Sure."

"Coffee would be great," he said.

"Trust me, it wouldn't," Trent assured him. "I'll take the hot chocolate."

Trent's comment bordered on rude but it was also true. I went to the kitchen, made two cups of delicious hot chocolate then filled a cup with hot water and added a coffee bag. I don't drink coffee, don't know how to make it, and see no need to learn. Paula does a great job at the restaurant. If not for her, I'd probably be serving hot water with coffee bags there too.

I carried the three cups to the living room. Trent occupied his usual spot on one end of my big, cushy sofa with brightly colored flowers, and Lawson sat stiffly erect in the faded rose colored recliner that doesn't match the sofa and I don't care. I handed out the beverages then sat beside Trent.

We all sipped in silence for a few moments. I didn't want to be the one to start talking about Bob. I didn't want to hear the awful words again or think about what had happened to him.

Henry appeared from the shadows and leapt onto the sofa. He settled beside me, a warm, fuzzy presence, and he didn't even mention catnip. He can be kind and caring, especially when he's well-fed and stoned.

Lawson set his cup on the coffee table. It was still half full of a murky brown liquid. He should have taken the hot chocolate. "So what can you tell us about Robert Markham?" he asked.

I set my own cup on the coffee table, pulled my feet up and wrapped my arms around my knees. "You can't find his home address because he didn't have one. He's—he was homeless."

Trent nodded. "We considered that possibility, but he was clean shaven, dressed in decent clothes."

I nodded and clutched my knees more tightly. "He was supposed to start a new job tomorrow. He was rebuilding his life." I told them about Bob's wife and his descent from successful businessman to homeless street person. "He was a good man. He just had some tough luck, but he was starting to get his life together again. This isn't fair." I blinked a couple of times and ordered myself not to cry, certainly not in front of the cops.

"Do you know where he was going to work?"

I shook my head. "Some construction company, an old friend of his. He called him Nick, but he didn't mention his last name and I didn't ask."

Trent and Lawson both made notes.

"Did he have any enemies?" Lawson asked.

I cringed, wishing I'd asked more questions, made more of an effort to find out about the unfortunate man who'd come and gone from my life in little more than the blink of an eye. "I don't know. I don't think so. He was a very nice person."

"How about friends?"

"I don't know. I didn't ask. I just gave him chocolate."

Trent slid closer and wrapped an arm around my shoulders. Maybe it wasn't strictly professional, but it felt really good. My boyfriend on one side, my cat on the other. I blinked fast and swallowed the lump rising in my throat.

"You did more than most people would have," Trent assured me. "It'll be all right. We'll make every effort to find out who killed your friend."

I nodded. Even if they caught the killer, that wouldn't help Bob.

"How..." I cleared my throat and forced myself to ask the question I didn't really want to know the answer to. "How did he die?"

"Blunt instrument," Lawson said bluntly.

Trent didn't elaborate and I didn't pursue the subject.

21

After a few more questions to which I had no answers, the boys gave up.

Lawson tucked his small notebook into his pocket. "Sorry we had to bring you bad news, Lindsay."

"Go ahead," Trent said to him. "I'll be there in a minute."

Lawson left and Trent pulled me into his arms. "Are you okay?"

I held on tight for an extra moment then stepped back and gave him my best *I'm tough* smile. "Absolutely."

"Want me to come back tonight after we file our reports?"

"Of course I want you to come back, but I'll be sound asleep when you get here. Might as well wait until we can be awake together this weekend."

"Call me if you need me." He gave me a quick kiss and left.

Henry and I went back to bed but suddenly I wasn't sleepy. Tired, exhausted and sad, but wide awake. I couldn't stop thinking of Bob and his proud smile as he told me about his new job. When the cops caught the creep who killed him, I hoped I'd have a chance to tell him what I thought of him. Actually, I hoped I'd have a chance to do more than that. Kick him in the crotch. Push him into a puddle of battery acid. Poke him in the eye with a sharp stick. Life had been unfair to Bob. Death had also been unfair.

I had just dozed off when the doorbell rang again. Henry opened one eye then closed it and continued his soft cat snores. He wasn't worried. Maybe Trent had returned.

I headed downstairs, not bothering to put on my jeans. If it was Trent, he'd seen me in less than my sleep shirt. If it wasn't Trent, I wouldn't open the door.

I flipped on the porch light and peered through the peephole.

It wasn't Trent.

It was some woman with smeared mascara, bright red hair and Big-D implants bulging out of a tiny tank top.

I live in a quiet neighborhood. Well, there was the time last month when that nut job tried to kill me in Sophie's house, but other than that, it's pretty quiet. Okay, for a while people were breaking into my house and digging up my basement. And Paula's ex did try to poison me. But my point is, I don't usually have hookers knocking on my door at midnight.

I turned around and headed back toward the stairs.

"Lindsay!"

The hooker knew my name.

And her voice sounded familiar.

Over the last couple of years of hanging with Fred, I'd met some interesting people. However, I would not invite most of them into my home in the middle of the night. I started up the stairs.

"Lindsay, you're no good for Rick!"

I froze in place with my hand on the stair rail and one foot on the bottom step. A red rose stuck in the door at work, a sleazy woman shouting my ex's name on my front porch in the middle of the night. Things were starting to fall into place.

"You're right!" I shouted back. "I'm terrible for him! You can have him. He's all yours! Good night!"

I made it up two more steps before the shrill voice stopped me again.

"Lindsay, we need to talk!"

"No, we don't."

"I could be a better mother to Rickie than you!"

I gasped. *Rickie?* The name struck fear through my heart and caused my whole body to tremble. I hadn't heard that name since his mother reclaimed him over a month ago. What ill wind had blown this woman to my front porch to utter that name in the middle of the night?

I went back downstairs and stood against the door. "Who are you and what do you want?"

"Lindsay, it's Ginger! Open the door!"

Ginger? Not a hooker, just a bimbo. I opened the door a crack. The woman didn't look like the Ginger I'd seen in Rick's house only a few weeks ago. "Ginger? Are you sure?"

"Of course I'm sure! Don't you remember me? I met you at Rick's last month."

The boobs were the same, but— "You were blond."

She bit her lip and wiped one eye, smudging the mascara further. Her eyes were blood shot as if she'd been crying. Or drinking. Or both. "You're a redhead. I thought he'd like me better if I looked like you."

Oh, good grief. "That was a very bad decision."

"He kicked me out! Yesterday we were talking about having a baby and tonight he kicked me out!"

"Yeah, Rick's not the fatherly type."

"Yes, he is! When he told Grace he was going to have a baby with me, she said she'd give him Rickie but only if he got back together with you. Grace likes you. Rickie likes you. Rick has to do it because that's his son and he missed the first years of his life, not because he loves you. It's all for his son."

I released a long sigh and dropped my head, uncertain how to respond to such a load of hogwash.

Ginger rushed into the gap of silence. "Rick says you're a good woman, but he's wrong. What kind of life do you think you're going to have, taking one woman's kid and another one's man?"

I could have told her Rick was lying, but it was the middle of the night and I didn't want to get into a pointless argument. "You're right," I said instead. "I won't do it. You keep Rick, and Grace can keep Rickie. Good night." I closed the door.

"Really?"

"Yes, really. You've made me see the error of my ways. Good night."

"Don't leave! I don't have anywhere to go. Rick kicked me out, and it's your fault."

Marrying a con artist is like grabbing hold of a sticky fly strip with both hands. Even when you finally manage to get it into the trash, you can never get all the sticky off your hands.

I was not going to take Ginger in for the night. I'd already provided B&B services for way too many of Rick's relatives and pseudo-relatives.

"There are lots of motels on the highway just a few miles away. I'd invite you to stay here, but I have a cat and Rick's allergic to cats, so if you go back to him all covered in cat hair, he'll go into anaphylactic shock and you'll have to take him to the hospital to get a shot in his genitals. You won't be able to have sex for five months. He might never be able to have kids after that." Yes, that was a load of hogwash too, but Rick set the standard.

"Really?" Ginger asked. "That's scary."

"Easily avoided. Find a motel. Good night. Live long and prosper."

I returned to bed. Henry opened one eye when I slid in beside him. I repeated the story I'd concocted about Rick's allergies and the possible consequences. He smiled and went back to sleep.

I actually slept better after Ginger left than before she came. The absurdity of the whole thing took my mind off Bob's death.

However, Henry woke me with his jungle-cat noises an hour later. He stood with his paws on the sill of the window, looking out at the street and making the noises he makes when someone he doesn't like comes around.

I wasn't even surprised at this third intrusion into my slumber.

I dragged myself out of bed and headed downstairs. Again. Henry marched alongside me.

Either the new visitor had catnip or my cat thought I needed protection.

What foul creature awaited me on my front porch? Rick? His son, Rickie? A zombie? Of the three, I was hoping for the zombie.

I peered through the peephole and saw no one, but Rickie's only nine years old so he's short. He could have been hiding.

Henry wasn't trying to claw through the front door so I assumed the visitor had probably left already.

Cautiously I eased the door open.

A huge bouquet of red roses waited on the porch.

Henry growled deep in his throat.

My thoughts exactly.

I stepped onto the porch and reached for the card. I had no doubt they were from Rickhead.

Henry growled again.

The noise sent shivers up my spine. I scanned my surroundings, looking for shadows in the moonlight, movement in the bushes, a figure darting behind somebody's house. Then I realized Henry was growling at the flowers.

I pulled the card from its plastic holder. By the romantic light of the full moon I read the words printed in messy block letters:

The first time I saw you,
Your eyes met mine,
And I knew you then
For all of time.
Your soul mate now and forever.
Oh, puke.

Chapter Three

I looked at the flowers. Huge moral dilemma.
Make a grand gesture and throw them in the trash or
take them inside and enjoy them without concern for
their origin? Strictly speaking, they originated from a
greenhouse. Rickhead's intervention between their
life on a rosebush and their appearance on my porch
didn't change the blooms in any material way.

I picked them up and started toward the door.

Henry growled again.

"Hey, the flowers are innocent! They didn't do
anything wrong."

He snorted, turned his back on me and went
upstairs.

I took the flowers to the kitchen and set them on
the table. The blossoms were lovely, untainted by
Rick's intrusion into their lives. The card, however,
was a different story.

I ripped it into tiny pieces, marched upstairs and
flushed it down the toilet.

Soul mate? Oh, please!

৯৵৹

The next morning when I pulled into the parking
lot behind Death by Chocolate, the street light
illuminated the yellow police tape surrounding a
chalk outline approximately where Bob had stood

28

when I handed him food and congratulated him the day before.

I got out of my car and walked through the predawn darkness to the outline. The crude drawing depicting a human form was empty and bore no resemblance to my friend. I wanted to hurry inside and not look, but I couldn't be a coward. Bob deserved better than that.

I slid under the yellow tape and stood beside the outline. An image of Bob lying there, dying alone and helpless, flashed across my mind. A dark puddle, black in the dim light, surrounded the head on the sketch.

I swallowed and forced myself to look more closely, to see if I could discern any clues in the outline, in the blood spatter pattern. I don't know anything about blood spatter patterns, but I felt certain Fred would. I took a picture with my cell phone.

"I'm glad I had the chance to know you, Bob." I hoped he could hear me.

I took a couple more pictures and went inside. I couldn't do anything else for Bob, and people would soon be needing chocolate.

Paula looked up from slathering butter onto the dough for cinnamon rolls. "Did you see the yellow tape and chalk outline in the alley?"

I nodded.

"Please tell me there hasn't been another murder."

I bit my lip and nodded again. "Bob."

Her eyes widened. "Bob? Our Bob?"

The words *our Bob* brought a weak smile to my lips. Paula isn't as detached as she'd like everybody to believe. "Yes, our Bob." I cleared my throat and tied on my apron, giving myself a minute to work up the courage to repeat what Trent had told me last night. "Blunt weapon. His head."

She drew in a deep breath and slowly released it then went back to buttering dough she'd already buttered. "Do they have any idea who did it?"

"I don't think so, but you know how Trent withholds information from me. I took some pictures of the crime scene. I'm going to send them to Fred to study and also have him see what he can find out about Bob's associates. Whoever did this will pay."

Paula was quiet for a long moment. "I'm sorry I called him *odd*."

"We can all be *odd* under the right circumstances. You were a little *odd* when I first met you."

She smiled. "Point taken." She went back to her cinnamon rolls.

I retrieved eggs, brown sugar, flour, butter, vanilla—all the ingredients for chocolate chip cookies. I also planned to make chocolate sheet cake, but the cookies were a staple, something I could make without thinking. "I have a happier story. Maybe it will help restore your faith in human nature." I told her about Brandon hitting my car, taking the blame and offering to give me a paint job for half price.

She slid a pan of rolls into the oven and looked at me, a frown creasing her forehead. "An automobile

30

accident is not exactly a warm and fuzzy, feel-good story. I hope you don't plan to trust your car to this man until you check him out."

Her faith in human nature remained blighted. "I gave Fred his card last night. By tonight I'll know everything about Mathis Paint and Body Shop, including what kind of toilet paper they use in the bathroom."

I refrained from telling Paula about the roses that appeared on my porch in the middle of the night. Not that I was keeping secrets, but I knew she'd narrow her eyes and think very loudly that I should have tossed them in the trash. I didn't want to talk about it. I planned to go home that evening and pretend the beautiful flowers had magically appeared on my kitchen table.

We finished with the breakfast crowd then made lunch, feeding chocolate to the masses. My chocolate sheet cake was a resounding success. When Brandon came in at the end of the lunch rush, I only had one piece left.

I greeted him with a big smile as he took a seat at the counter. Again he wore a clean sh irt and jeans. Either he was a meticulous painter or he changed clothes before he left work even at lunch. "Good afternoon!" I set a glass of water in front of him. "Nice to see you under more pleasant circumstances, Brandon."

He returned my smile and even blushed slightly. Cute. People love it when you remember their name. "Hi, Lindsay. It's nice to see you too."

"Can I interest you in a corned beef sandwich or maybe a slice of quiche and a bowl of tomato soup?"

"Corned beef sounds good." He looked at the chalk board on the wall behind me. "And a piece of chocolate sheet cake. I can't wait to try it."

"You're in luck. I have only one left." I set the last piece in front of him.

His smile widened. "The last piece? You saved it for me?"

"I did. I'll get that sandwich to you shortly."

I came around the counter and headed toward a customer sending chocolate vibes.

"So we're okay?" Brandon asked. "You've forgiven me for denting your car?"

"Of course," I called over my shoulder. "Can I get you some dessert, sir?"

Brandon dallied over his dessert until the last customer left. Paula gave him a meaningful look, a *Hurry up and finish so we can close look.* I introduced them, they did the *Pleased to meet you* thing, and Paula took a load of dirty dishes to the kitchen.

"So," I said, "hope to see you in here again tomorrow." *I can't see you again until I no longer see you now.*

He smiled. "I'll be here." He took three colored cards from his pocket and spread them on the counter. "I need your opinion. I think this one—" he indicated the card in the middle— "would be perfect for your car, but these other two are also nice shades of red."

He was right. All three colors were great, much brighter than my car's faded hue, but the middle one screamed *speed*.

He slid the cards toward me. "Take them with you. Think about it."

I picked up the color samples. "You pretty much nailed it."

A wide grin spread across his pleasant face. "Come by the shop when you close here. I'll work up an estimate, and I promise you'll be happy with the numbers."

I nodded. "I'll be there." Going in for an estimate wasn't making a commitment. I wouldn't do that until I heard back from Fred, though I was impressed with Brandon's ability to choose exactly the right color.

He put some bills on the counter beside the check. "I'll be waiting."

He left and I locked up behind him then gathered the remaining dishes and headed back to the kitchen.

Paula stood at the sink rinsing plates.

"Look at this." I held the red cards in front of her. "What do you think about one of these for my car?"

Paula gave the colors a cursory glance. "You don't think you're visible enough to the traffic cops already?"

I snorted. "That's a myth about red cars getting more tickets. I got just as many tickets when I had a silver car."

"Did Brandon bring those to you?"

"Yeah. I'm going to take my car by his shop after work and let him give me an estimate."

Paula frowned. "He seems nice enough, but you don't really know anything about him."

I rolled my eyes. "I know about my car. It already has a lot of dents and scrapes. You think he's going to somehow make it worse? Didn't we just have a discussion this morning about how suspicious and cynical you are, and you admitted you were wrong?"

"No, we did not. I admitted I shouldn't have called Bob *odd*. That does not qualify as a discussion or an admission of the error of my ways."

I shrugged. "Okay, maybe I was paraphrasing. But you are way too suspicious and cynical." I could have pointed out that her suspicious attitude had almost caused her to lose the new man in her life, Matthew, but since their relationship was still tentative, I decided to keep my mouth shut on that one. For the moment.

"And you're too trusting" she accused. "Call Fred and get his report before you go over there."

I slid the color cards into my jeans pocket. "Yeah, yeah, yeah."

I did call Fred as soon as we had the restaurant cleaned up and ready to open in the morning.

"Sorry about Bob," he said.

"How did you know about Bob? Have you got my house bugged?"

"Don't be silly." I noticed he didn't deny it. "When Detectives Trent and Lawson showed up at your door in the middle of the night, I knew something was going on so I checked the police reports. Robert Markham, murdered in the alley behind Death by Chocolate. Had to be your friend Bob."

He made it all sound so normal and innocuous. There's nothing normal or innocuous about Fred. Either he has the entire neighborhood—maybe the entire city—bugged or he has supernatural powers.

"I took pictures of the crime scene. I thought you could analyze the blood spatter pattern."

"You've been watching *CSI* again, haven't you?"

"*Dexter*, actually. Your surveillance is slipping if you didn't know that."

"No, I'm not going to analyze the blood spatter pattern."

I heaved a sigh of deep frustration. "Can you at least find out who Bob associated with? You could start with finding out Nick's last name. Nick's the guy who offered him a job. Then we can question him and see if he knows who might have wanted Bob dead."

"Lindsay, life on the streets is tough." Fred's voice was uncommonly gentle. "Bob was living in a dangerous world. We may never know who killed him."

"I can't believe you have such a defeatist attitude. Do you want chocolate tonight or not?"

"Since you put it that way, I'll see what I can find out, but it may not be much."

"I knew I could count on you. Now, about Mathis Paint and Body Shop...will my car be safe in their hands?"

"I think it may be a little late to start worrying about your car's safety, but Mathis Paint and Body appears to be reputable. They've been in operation for twenty-three years and have several four and five star customer reviews."

"Great! Thanks! I'll bring you chocolate when I get home."

"Wait a minute. There's more. The one bad review I found was about the owner's attitude, the father. A female customer accused him of sexual harassment."

"Ewww. Well, I'm dealing with the son, not the father."

"And the father has two DUIs on his driving record."

"So the guy's made a couple of mistakes. We're all entitled to a few of those. I married Rick. Paula married David. I bet even you made a mistake or two in your life, didn't you?"

He ignored my probing question. "The son, Brandon, is clean. He doesn't seem to have inherited his father's tendency to get into trouble. He's twenty-four years old and still lives at home. Mother died five years ago. Brandon has worked in the family business since he graduated from high school. Nothing on his record, not even a speeding ticket."

"That sounds a little suspicious. I'm not sure I trust somebody who's never had a speeding ticket, but maybe he's just never been caught."

"Let me know when you get ready to take your car in, and I'll go with you."

"Okay." That's my code word for: *It's okay for you to think that and I'm not going to argue with you, but I'm going to do as I please.* "Thanks for the information. I'll send you the pictures I took of the crime scene right now and bring you chocolate later tonight."

Paula and I finished cleaning then I drove the two miles to Mathis Paint and Body Shop with visions of a shiny new paint job dancing in my head. The place was on a side street, bordered on the right by an automobile salvage yard and on the left by a rundown storage facility. A good location. Handy parts and no one around to complain about the noise and paint fumes.

I pulled up to the open entrance and stopped.

A space alien wearing beige coveralls and a plastic helmet of some sort came out to greet me. The alien lifted the plastic shield off Brandon's face. "Hi, Lindsay. You can come on in. I've already cleared a space for you." He indicated the right side of the open doorway.

I drove into the structure and got out. Half a dozen cars in various stages of repair from crunched like an accordion to smooth and shiny occupied bays along the length of the structure. Obviously a legitimate business. I made a mental note to tell Paula her suspicions were once again unfounded.

Brandon came over to join me. "I'm so glad you made it." The coveralls were spotted and stained. That was reassuring too, explained how he could stay so clean when he was doing a dirty job.

I waved a hand toward my battered but beautiful car. "What do you think? Can you make her look all shiny and new?"

"It will be my pleasure. Why don't you have a seat in the office? It's air conditioned." He indicated a small cubicle in the back. "I'll have a look at this gem and see what we can do with her."

"Works for me." I started toward the office.

An older man emerged from another room in the back. His father? He was a little shorter than Brandon but had the same brown hair and eyes. I could see a faint resemblance, but the older man was muscular and rough with pock-marked skin and bushy brows low over narrow eyes. He looked vaguely familiar— maybe because he looked like Brandon or maybe I'd seen him in Death by Chocolate before.

When he saw me, he smiled, but the expression didn't improve his appearance. I could see this man collecting DUIs and getting accused of sexual harassment. "Can I help you?" he asked.

"Brandon's looking at my car." I motioned toward my vehicle where Brandon stood, his face expressionless, watching us. "Paint job."

"Well, you've brought it to the right place. I'm Grady Mathis, the owner here." He extended a calloused hand.

"I'm Lindsay Powell. Nice to meet you." I accepted his hand and immediately wished for a Handi Wipe.

I was overreacting. The man's hand was clean and dry. I forced a smile and gave myself a mental slap. Grady Mathis was being polite. If Fred hadn't told me about his background, I'd probably have thought he was a perfectly nice man.

Or not.

"We'll take good care of you, Lindsay."

I flinched. Why did he say *we'll take good care of you* and not *we'll take good care of your car*?

Why was I being so silly? "Good. Great. I'll just wait in here."

I fled to the small office, dropped onto the cracked vinyl covered seat of one of the two chairs and picked up a tattered *People* magazine. I opened it but didn't look at the pages. Instead I watched Grady Mathis walk toward Brandon where he stood beside my car, making notes on a clipboard. Brandon looked up and the two men started talking.

I should have closed the door. I didn't. Instead I strained to hear what they were saying. Pretty boring. Not worth the effort expended. A lot of technical terms about repairing the dents in my car and how the paint job should be done.

Then the subject of cost came up and Brandon told him the deal he'd struck with me. The older Mathis' voice got really low and I could no longer hear even the occasional word. However, I could tell from his tone that he was angry. Darn! Suddenly I felt guilty. Yes, guilty because somebody hit my car.

When Mathis shoved Brandon, I'd had enough.

I dropped all pretense of looking at the magazine and marched toward them. The conversation ceased and both men looked at me. Brandon smiled tentatively and his father leered.

"My car seems to be causing a problem. I think I'd better take it somewhere else. Brandon, I appreciate your offer, but this isn't a good idea."

I reached for the door handle but Grady Mathis stepped in front of me. "I'm sorry you had to hear our family problems," he said. "My fault. My boy screwed up and he's trying to make it right. I'd appreciate it if you'd let us do that."

"Please." Brandon's voice was small like that of a child. I felt a rush of sympathy for him. Obviously his father was a bully. No wonder Brandon seemed so meek and grateful for every kind word. Probably didn't get many of them at home. I'd have to pay more attention to him and give him a little extra chocolate from time to time.

In the meantime, I'd get the estimate and get out of that place as fast as I could. I looked at my watch. "Okay, but I have an appointment in half an hour." That was the truth. An appointment to feed my cat. Henry would be starving by the time I got home.

"No problem," Mathis assured me. "Have a seat. We'll get right on it."

I returned to the small room and the *People* magazine while Brandon checked out every inch of my car. Grady Mathis stayed with him a few minutes then came over to stand in the doorway of the office, thick arms crossed over his thick chest. "Sorry about that little scene."

I pretended to be absorbed in the celebrity pictures in the magazine. "It's okay. None of my business."

"Brandon's a good kid. Just needs a firm hand."

"He seems like a very nice young man." I emphasized the last two words.

Brandon appeared behind his father. "Got your estimate finished."

I rose and took the paper from his hand. "Thank you. I'll be in touch."

For a moment I stood motionless waiting for the elder Mathis to move out of my way. I couldn't get through the door without touching him, and that wasn't going to happen.

Finally he smiled and stepped back. "Look forward to seeing you again soon."

I bared my teeth at him and hoped he took the expression for what it was—a threat, not a smile.

Brandon followed me to my car and opened the door. "Don't let my dad upset you. He's okay, just a few rough edges."

"He seems pretty hard on you."

Brandon dropped his head. "Sometimes, I guess. My mom died a few years ago and I'm all he's got left."

"I'm sorry."

Brandon lifted his gaze again. "It means a lot that you're willing to let me fix your car and make up for what I did to you."

Oh, great. Another guilt trip. Pack my bags and grab my passport.

I drove straight home, desperate to reach the serenity of my house and have a glass of wine. I was beyond the chocolate and Coke stage. I needed alcohol. And maybe a little chocolate.

Henry greeted me at the door, and I could feel my stress level dropping as he wound himself around my legs and purred.

I headed straight for the kitchen with him trotting at my heels. "You're not going to believe the day I had." He purred reassuringly. He's such a good listener.

I stopped in the kitchen doorway and gasped in horror at the specks of red that covered the table and floor and even some of the cabinets. Bits and pieces of rose petals. Some evil creature had shredded my beautiful flowers.

"Henry!"

He looked up, wide blue eyes innocent. But his paws had red stains.

Chapter Four

I studied my guilty cat who didn't look the least bit guilty. In fact, he looked quite pleased with himself.

"I get it," I said. "I understand what you're trying to say. I understand the flowers were tainted. But who's going to clean up this mess?"

We both knew who was going to clean up that mess.

He strolled over to the drawer where I kept the catnip, looked up and meowed.

"Really? Okay, I'm not going to kill you for this, but I'm certainly not going to reward you!"

I cleaned up the shredded flowers, fed Henry and baked some chocolate chip cookies for Fred. I did *not* give Henry catnip.

When I walked out the door with the cookies, I saw Sophie in white shorts and a white shirt coming out of Fred's house. It was seven o'clock in the evening. Not really a suspicious time. But I was suspicious. More talk about her financial affairs? Ha!

She saw me and waved. Henry and I hurried over, catching up to her at the end of the sidewalk. Henry gave her a head butt on the leg, and she reached down to pet him.

"How's the decorating business going?" I asked.

She smiled. Was she blushing? Hard to tell with her olive skin. When I blush, it lights up the room. "Business is good," she said. "I signed another new client today. How are chocolate sales?"

"Good." I searched my mind for something to say besides…*What were you and Fred doing? Of course it's none of my business, but tell me anyway because I'm nosy.* The only thing that came to mind, the thing that I couldn't seem to get out of my mind, was Bob's murder. "Did you hear about my friend who got killed in the alley behind my restaurant?"

She nodded. "I'm so sorry. Fred told me how much you did for the poor man. That was very kind of you."

I don't often get accused of being *kind*. I shrugged. "I just gave him some leftovers. He was the one who struggled to get his life back together. So what else did Fred say?"

She waved a hand as if whatever he'd said was inconsequential. "Oh, you know Fred."

I wasn't sure I did. "Drop by sometime and we'll have a glass of wine and some chocolate." A couple of glasses of wine. Get her tipsy and maybe she'd open up and spill her guts.

"Sounds like fun." She smiled and headed across the street toward her house.

I watched her for a moment, but it's just as difficult to read minds from the back as it is from the front. Henry and I turned and went up Fred's walk.

When we reached Fred's immaculate flowerbeds with chrysanthemums and dahlias and moonflower vines and other flowers I can't identify, I stopped and glared at Henry. "You got away with eating my flowers, but don't get any ideas about touching Fred's. Some of these are deadly nightshade." They might have been for all I knew.

He gave me a haughty look and strolled away.

"And don't come home with mouse fur between your teeth!" I understand it's the thought that counts, but I just can't work up the proper appreciation for his little gifts, and they were becoming more frequent as fall approached.

"Are you talking to yourself or to my flowers?"

I looked up at the sound of Fred's voice.

"I was talking to..." Henry was gone. "Do you want these cookies or not?"

"Of course." Fred held the door open.

I gave his flowers a final glance. There were no wilted leaves or petals in sight. Fred's garden elf cleans them all up in the middle of the night.

"I expect to open the door one morning and find Henry with an elf in his mouth." I handed him the plastic container of cookies and strode into his living room.

"An elf? Are these laced with something other than nuts?"

"Yes, real vanilla. You have lipstick on your shirt."

He looked down at his immaculate white cotton shirt. "No, I don't."

"You had to check to be sure."

He set the container of cookies on the coffee table. "I'm going to open a bottle of wine. Would you like a glass or have you already had your limit?"

"After the last twenty-four hours, you don't have enough wine to reach my limit."

Fred disappeared into the kitchen, and I looked around the room carefully, searching for evidence of what he and Sophie had been doing.

No dust was disturbed on his oak coffee table because there was no dust. The bottoms of his mini blinds were all completely level. Every grain of wood was in place on his hardwood floor. The leather of his sofa and recliner was smooth and showed no signs of human habitation.

"What are you doing?"

I looked up from my close examination of the sofa to see Fred approaching with a bottle of wine and two glasses.

When faced with a question I don't want to answer, I've found the best response is to change the subject. "What did you find out about Bob?"

Fred set the glasses on his coffee table and filled them with red wine then sat in his recliner. Actually, he filled his halfway and mine almost to the brim. "The company your friend was going to work for is A-Plus Construction owned by Nicholas Peterson."

I picked up my glass, sat on the pristine sofa and took a big gulp of wine. Hearing the name of a real company made Bob's death even more real, as real as if I'd seen the body. "This Nicholas Peterson, does he have a record?"

"He's had a few speeding tickets, if that makes you feel better about him, but nothing else. Married to the same woman for thirty years, two daughters, three grandchildren. His colleagues respect him."

"If Bob had his own construction company, then the two of them would have been business rivals. That could be a motive. Peterson might have been afraid Bob would make a strong comeback, set up on his own again and threaten his company."

Fred shook his head. "I don't think so. From what I've been able to find, they were always friends. Worked together on a lot of projects."

I took another sip of wine. "Hmmph. Peterson reentered Bob's life after all this time, and now Bob's dead. Doesn't that sound like an awfully big coincidence to you?"

"The police interviewed him today, and they don't consider him a person of interest." His voice went soft, the way it had when we'd talked on the phone earlier. I liked it much better when he was haughty and sarcastic. "Lindsay, you may never know what happened to your friend. This was likely a random attack. He was cleaned up and wearing decent clothes. Somebody may have thought he had money so they killed him for it."

"He would have had money again and a nice home and maybe another wife. But whoever did this didn't give him a chance. I don't believe it was a robbery gone bad, but even if it was, we have to find who did it."

Fred rose from his chair and came over to me. He produced a tissue and offered it to me.

47

I sniffed. "I don't need that."

"Would you like more wine?"

I looked at my glass and found it mysteriously empty. "Sure."

He laid the tissue beside me and refilled my glass then went back to his chair.

"Did you have a chance to look over the pictures I sent you?" I asked.

He nodded. "The victim appears to have been standing when someone came up behind him. He started to turn, but the attacker hit him on the side of the head with a blunt instrument."

"I'm impressed that you can tell all that from the blood spatter pattern in those pictures."

"That and the pictures of the body in situ that the police took."

I wasn't surprised that he'd hacked into the police department's records. Or maybe he didn't hack. Maybe he worked for them.

Day trader? Financial analyst? Not likely.

"So where do we go from here?" I asked. "I think we should question Nicholas Peterson. That's the only lead we have."

Fred's brows drew together in a frown. "It's not a very good lead. The police interview yielded nothing. You may have to let them handle this one. They have resources we don't."

I glared at him, took another sip of wine, and leaned back on the sofa. "You have just as many or more resources than they do, and I have something on my side that none of you do. I cared about Bob. I want his murderer caught. To the cops, he's just another street person in the wrong place at the wrong time. To me, he was a friend, somebody who mattered. If you won't help, I'll do it by myself."

"Do what? Talk to the man who was going to give Bob another chance by hiring him? What do you think he's going to tell you?"

"I guess I won't know until I talk to him. He might be able to give me names of Bob's enemies."

"He told the police he didn't know anybody who'd want to hurt Bob."

"But you have ways to get information out of people that the police don't."

Fred sipped his wine in silence for a couple of minutes. "I think this was a random murder, not something personal."

He doesn't like to admit when he's wrong, but I could tell he was hooked. "You *think* that, but you're not sure. I do have a point, don't I?"

He rolled his eyes and sipped his wine. Definitely interested.

"We could catch Peterson at work tomorrow," I said. "Talk to him, look around to see who else is there and whose ears perk up at the mention of Bob's name."

"I'll do some checking and see if I can find anything to go on. If I can't, you have to agree to let it go. Deal?"

We were practically on our way to A-Plus Construction. "Deal."

"Tell me how your trip to the Mathis Paint and Body Shop went."

I set down my wine. "What makes you think I went there? Do you have me micro-chipped?"

"When we talked earlier today and I offered to go with you to take your car in, you said, *Okay*. That means you don't want to talk about it anymore but you're going to do as you please and not comply with whatever's being requested of you."

Busted! He broke the code!

I told him about my visit to the Mathis Paint and Body Shop.

He opened the container of cookies and carefully selected the most symmetrical one. "I don't like the sound of those people. I hope you're not planning to take your car back."

"No. Of course not." I twirled my glass and watched the crimson liquid swirl around the curved crystal sides. "Probably not. I mean, I do feel sorry for Brandon, and I think it would help him if he could personally do something to repair the damage he did to my car. They did offer me a really good price. And Brandon has a color picked out for my car that's absolutely perfect."

"I don't think that's a good idea. I don't like the idea of you doing business with somebody like Grady Mathis. I'll talk to the man who works on my car. He'll give you a decent price and do a good job, and he isn't a pervert."

"Okay."

He looked at me. He didn't move a muscle, didn't frown, didn't scrunch his lips or narrow his eyes, but I knew what he was thinking. He'd broken the code. He knew the translation of *okay*. I tried to stare him down but finally gave up.

"All right!" I threw up my hands in submission. "I won't take my car back to the Mathis boys. Do you want me to put that in writing and get it notarized?"

"If you'd like."

"I wouldn't." I set my empty glass on the coffee table and stood. "I'm going home. I didn't get much sleep last night. With any sort of luck, I won't be interrupted by the cops or Rick's girlfriend tonight."

"Rick's girlfriend?"

"Aha! You don't see everything!" I told him about Ginger's late-night visit and the bouquet of roses that Henry destroyed.

He frowned. "I don't like the sound of either of those events."

I shrugged. "It's irritating but it's no big deal. Just Rickhead dumping another woman. He probably has number seventy-three waiting in the wings."

Both sides of Fred's mouth slid upward in a grin. "Seventy-three? Have you been keeping track?"

"You know I'm not good with numbers. It could be seventy-four."

"I'll keep an eye on your house in case you have any more late night visitations."

"You have my permission to shoot anybody who comes to my door tonight."

He arched a well-groomed eyebrow. "Anybody?"

"Well, not Trent and not Paula or Zach, but anybody else."

"In other words, it's okay if I shoot Rick."

"I'll help you hide the body." Like Fred would need any help.

He walked me outside and I started down the steps toward the sidewalk. It was dark and I'd had two glasses of wine so I thought I should stick to the sidewalk rather than going cross country through my yard with its irregular patches of grass and a few mole holes.

I turned back on the bottom step of his porch. "I saw Sophie leaving when I came over. More work on her financial affairs?" Yes, it was none of my business, but it never hurts to ask. Worst that can happen is the other person will lie or just won't answer.

"Yes."

It was possible. Not likely, but possible.

I went home and Henry met me at the door with a small furry gift. "Thank you." I forced a smile. *It's the thought that counts.*

He laid the little mouse body at my feet and sauntered inside. I followed him and retrieved a plastic bag from the kitchen then returned to the porch and scooped Henry's gift into the bag. I'd buried the first ones he brought home but realized early on that I'd run out of yard before Henry ran out of mice. I carried the evening's gift to the trash can and tossed it in. "Rest in peace," I said and closed the lid.

When I went back inside Henry was waiting at the bottom of the stairs. He gave me a questioning look.

"It was delicious. Thank you."

Apparently happy with that answer, he went upstairs to the bedroom.

My sleep that night was uninterrupted. I woke with the alarm and got up without hitting the snooze button even once.

৵৽

When I pulled into the alley behind Death by Chocolate the next morning, I noticed that the crime scene tape was gone. I was glad I didn't have to see it, but I wondered if that meant the cops had stopped working on the case, if it had gone cold already.

I parked and headed for the door. The windows of the shop were dark. That meant I was there before Paula, something that didn't happen very often.

I fumbled with my keys as I approached the door, trying to find the right one, and stumbled over something.

My heart rate accelerated to roughly the speed of light. I grabbed at the door handle to steady myself.

What had I tripped over? What lay in front of the door to my shop? I didn't want to look down. Logic told me it was not another body. It was too small for that. But standing in a dark alley at three forty-five in the morning was not conducive to logical thinking.

I gritted my teeth, closed my eyes and looked down. Okay, I guess it didn't count as *looking* when my eyes were closed. I forced them open, forced myself to look at the object lying at my feet.

It was a bottle of wine. Red Head Merlot.

And a note attached with a piece of ribbon.

I was furious—with myself for being terrified by a bottle of wine and with Rickhead for leaving it there.

I didn't hesitate. I marched over to the dumpster and tossed in the bottle and the note. The bottle hit the bottom with a satisfying crash.

When it came to gifts, I preferred Henry's dead mice to Rickhead's offerings.

Chapter Five

When Paula arrived ten minutes later, I was making cookies and fuming about Rick's latest intrusion into my life. I told her the whole story, including the roses, the fact that I'd actually planned to keep them, and how Henry had disagreed and disposed of them.

She kneaded and rolled dough quietly, allowing me to rant until I finally wound down. I shoved a pan of chocolate chip cookies into the oven and slammed the door. "I'm going to call and tell him he had better back off! No, I'm going to go to his house and threaten to beat him with my iron skillet if he doesn't leave me alone!"

Paula calmly spread butter over her dough. "I don't think that's a good idea. That's what he wants. Your attention. You should just ignore him. After all, it doesn't hurt anything if he leaves gifts and notes at your home and work."

"*Doesn't hurt anything?* Excuse me? I nearly had a heart attack this morning!"

"If you'd been paying attention to where you were going, you would have seen the wine and you wouldn't have been frightened. If he leaves anything else, throw it away and forget it. Ignoring Rick is the cruelest thing you can do to him."

I opened my mouth to protest. I was angry. I didn't want to just forget it. I wanted to take some kind of action. Recycle Henry's furry gifts to Rick's front door. Send Fred after him with a machine gun...again.

But, much as I hated to admit it, Paula had a point.

I threw my pot holder onto the counter. "Fine. I'll just freaking forget it. Let him get away with being a stalker."

Paula knows me too well. She recognized my grudging capitulation for what it was...capitulation. She ignored the *grudging* part. "That's wise. Don't give him the satisfaction of knowing he got your attention."

I felt angry all over again, this time at myself for getting sucked into his game. I marched back to the counter and took out the ingredients for chocolate marshmallow pudding. "He will call eventually, you know."

"Maybe, or maybe he'll get diverted by another woman before that happens." She looked up and smiled. "But if he leaves you any of those Christopher Elbow Artisan Chocolates he used to bring, you can always re-gift them to me."

Paula was right. I hate it when that happens. I was letting Rick get to me. If he left gifts in the middle of the night and ran away without so much as ringing my doorbell, no harm done. If he left more flowers, I'd bring them to the shop instead of leaving them home with Henry. I regretted tossing the wine.

Rick had expensive taste. It was probably a very nice wine.

But if he left me chocolates, I'd have to eat those. It's a crime—a felony, I think—to waste chocolate, especially Christopher Elbow Artisan Chocolates.

I tried to put Rick out of my mind and focus on measuring, stirring, whipping, and, of course, taste-testing my desserts for the day. I wanted to get everything done as quickly as possible so I could leave early and get to A-Plus Construction before it closed. I felt certain Fred would go with me, but if he didn't, I would do it anyway. I knew the routine. I could do it on my own if I had to.

We were crazy busy with the breakfast crowd when the business phone rang. Paula was standing at the register, ringing up a customer, so she grabbed it with one hand while handing the man his change with the other.

I was across the room refilling coffees, but I could almost feel the force of her gaze. I turned and saw that her eyes were narrowed and her lips thinned. Had to be her ex-husband or mine. Hers was in prison.

She mouthed, "Rick."

I shook my head and filled another coffee cup. Darn. I'd been hoping he'd leave the chocolates before his ghost gifting ran its course.

I crossed the room, returned the empty coffee pot to its place and picked up the full one.

"He wants you to call him." Paula took the full pot from me. "He says it's important."

"Really? Important to who? Not to me."

She frowned and looked unusually serious. "He sounded rattled."

I shrugged. "Sounding rattled is part of his salesman's persona. He uses it on an as-need basis."

A new customer sat down at the counter and I went over to take his order.

Rick called again an hour later when we were preparing for the lunch crowd. Unfortunately I answered the phone.

"Lindsay—"

"I'm busy! Do I call you at work?"

"Please, I need to talk to you." He sounded frantic. He does *frantic* just as well as he does rattled, charming, sad, pitiful, interested…the appropriate emotion for the moment. "It's about Ginger!"

"I know all about Ginger. She came by my house night before last. I can't believe you told her you and I are getting back together. Why can't you ever be honest? Why couldn't you just tell her you'd found somebody else? You are the lowest kind of scum!"

"I can explain!"

Across the room I saw a customer look up from his menu. I had to get back to business. I hated to be rude so I said, "Have a nice day. Goodbye," before I slammed the phone down. One must observe the civilities.

❧

There's something invigorating about the busy times. We rush through the cycle of serving food, clearing tables and serving food again. It requires an intense focus, complete concentration on every customer's progress and needs. I was in the zone, bringing happiness and chocolate to the lunch crowd. That's my only excuse for failing to notice Grady Mathis sitting at the counter until he spoke to me.

"I'm here for the best chocolate in town." He grinned and winked.

Though it was an innocuous statement, he made it sound lascivious.

I waved a hand at the menu on the chalkboard behind me. "Today's special dessert is chocolate marshmallow pudding." I almost bit my tongue for telling him. If he got the pudding, he'd eat it from a dish using a spoon. I wasn't sure I'd be able to get either the dish or the spoon clean again. "We always have brownies with and without nuts and chocolate chip cookies with and without nuts. We're famous for the chocolate chip cookies with nuts." *Please get the cookies!*

"Then I'll have the turkey sandwich, French fries, a glass of tea, and two chocolate chip cookies." He winked again. "With nuts."

"Coming right up." I turned away to fill his order…and to breathe air he hadn't breathed.

Poor Brandon! And now his disgusting father had even invaded his chocolate space. If he came in at his usual time, that would leave an hour for Grady Mathis to eat and leave. It would not be a good thing for both of them to be there at the same time.

By one thirty the crowd had thinned and the senior Mathis still sat at the counter sipping his third glass of tea and making stupid comments every time I got close. I gave him the check when I gave him his food, but he didn't take the hint.

I thought about asking Paula to cover the counter but was concerned he'd be just as obnoxious to her. I figured I could handle it better. I have the ability to be a little obnoxious myself when the occasion calls for it. Unfortunately, Mathis took everything I said as a joke and seemed to think I was being flirtatious. I quit responding and did my best to avoid him.

Finally he pushed his ticket and a twenty dollar bill across the counter. I snatched it up and went to get his change.

"So when are you bringing that hot car in for me to work on?" he asked.

I plunked his change down on the counter in front of him. "I'm not sure. I need to coordinate my schedule with my boyfriend, Detective Adam Trent." When sarcasm fails, play the cop card.

Mathis lifted a shaggy eyebrow and grinned. Actually, it was closer to a leer than a grin. "Got a cop for a boyfriend, eh? You are a feisty little thing!"

I am neither little nor feisty, but I let it go. "Excuse me. I think someone needs chocolate." Though I didn't see any particular person signaling for dessert, everyone always needs chocolate. I took a brownie from the display case and strode across the room.

I met Paula as she headed for the kitchen with a tray of dirty dishes. She looked at the brownie, at me and then in Grady Mathis' direction. "Table four could use a complimentary dessert." Paula's practically psychic. Sometimes that's a good thing, and sometimes it's downright annoying. In this particular instance, I was glad.

I took the brownie to table four and presented it to the quiet, fortyish lady who dined with us so often I actually remembered her face. She looked up from her book when I approached.

I smiled. "Compliments of the house. To thank you for being a loyal customer."

She returned my smile and blushed. "Why, thank you!"

A good thing had come out of Grady Mathis' visit.

I heard the bell over the door and turned to see if he was leaving.

Brandon came in.

I could tell the moment he saw his father. He stopped in midstride and his face turned dark and stormy. Damn. Were we going to have a shootout at the Chocolate Corral?

Brandon drew in a deep breath, continued toward the counter and took a seat next to his father.

Grady Mathis slid off his stool and slapped his son on the back. "Good choice. Enjoyed the food. See you back at work." He sauntered across the room.

I watched him the same way I watch the occasional snake slithering across my yard...creeped out but unable to look away. I shouldn't have done that. He paused at the door, saw me looking, pointed a finger gun at me, grinned and winked.

That broke the spell. I spun away and returned to the counter. "Hey, Brandon. Good to see you. How does a BLT sound today?"

His lips were compressed into a thin line, his eyes dark, angry slits. "What did he want?"

I spread my hands. "It's a restaurant. He came in to eat."

"What did he say?"

I did not want to contribute to a fight between father and son. Wouldn't bother me if I contributed to a fight between Trent and Grady Mathis or Fred and Grady Mathis. I'd enjoy seeing the slaughter. But I didn't want to make Brandon's life worse. "He said he wanted a turkey sandwich, French fries, a glass of tea and two chocolate chip cookies."

"And you gave it to him?"

Brandon and his father did not have a storybook father-son relationship, and I was on Brandon's side. However, I wasn't going to let my restaurant become a battleground for the two of them. "Of course I gave it to him. That's what I do here. I serve food to anybody who comes through the door. I'd even serve my ex-husband if he came in, though I might have to put a little cyanide in his iced tea."

Brandon smiled. Crisis averted. "Yeah, okay, I'll have the BLT, an iced tea, and whatever your special dessert is today."

"Chocolate marshmallow pudding." I caught my eye halfway through a wink. Oh no! Was obnoxicity contagious? I hurried to the kitchen to put together Brandon's order. Feeling irrationally guilty for serving his father, I added an extra piece of bacon to his sandwich. Bacon runs a close second to chocolate when it comes to soothing the troubled soul.

Paula came in with another load of dishes. "What was that little drama all about? Who was that disgusting man?"

"Brandon's father. Owner of Mathis Paint and Body. I gave Brandon an extra piece of bacon."

Paula turned on the faucet in the sink to rinse the dishes. "With a father like that, he's going to need all the extra bacon he can get."

I took Brandon's sandwich and iced tea to him.

The place was quiet, only a few people left, so I lingered to chat with him, give him that extra bit of attention. "How's the sandwich?"

"Very good. My favorite sandwich. Everything you make here is great."

"Thank you, but I have to give Paula credit for cooking the bacon. I'm just the chocolatier."

He smiled. "The best one in the world."

"That might be overstating it. Maybe the best in the city. Well, the country. Okay, I'm good with *best in the world*."

The front door burst open and Rick charged inside, his blond hair wild, his eyes wide. His tie was even askew.

That's what always happens when I ignore Rick. He shows up at my front door or, on one occasion, in my shower.

What had I just been saying about serving my ex-husband? And me fresh out of cyanide.

He strode up to the counter and slammed his hands down. "Damn it, Lindsay, when I call you at work, it's because it's important! Don't just blow me off!"

I forced myself to remain calm. There were still a few people in the restaurant. If I killed him, a chocolatier with blood on her hands would probably not increase sales for desserts made with those hands. "You have my attention. What is this important matter you want to talk to me about?"

He ran a hand distractedly through his hair and swallowed. "Ginger's been murdered."

Chapter Six

My chin dropped. "Are you sure?" I cringed as I heard the silly question come out of my mouth.

"Of course I'm sure," he snapped. "I found her body."

If attention was what he wanted, he had it—my attention and that of the few people left in the restaurant.

Paula came out from the kitchen and stood beside me.

"Did you hear?" Rick asked her, his voice a loud wail. "Ginger's dead!"

"I heard," Paula said quietly. "I'll take over out here. You two can go in the back and talk."

I walked around the counter and took Rick's arm. "Let's go to the kitchen."

He threw himself at me, wrapped his arms around me and made huge gulping noises. If I hadn't known him better, I might have thought he was crying.

I patted his shoulder and tried to disentangle myself while moving us closer to the kitchen door.

"It's my fault!" he pseudo-sobbed. "I broke up with her!"

"Breaking up with her got her murdered?" I pushed against the kitchen door with one hand and dragged Rick through with the other.

65

"She killed herself because of me!"

When the kitchen door swung shut behind us, I shoved him away. "Suicide?" She had been pretty distraught when she'd come to my door. I supposed it was possible a woman could kill herself over Rick. It's also possible the Easter Bunny lays colored eggs and leaves them under the Christmas tree for good children to find. "I thought you said she was murdered. How did she die? If she was stabbed fifty-seven times, suicide is unlikely."

He reached for my hand. I put both of them behind my back and moved away from him.

He rubbed his eyes with a thumb and forefinger. "It was awful."

I had no doubt it was awful, but it was hard to feel sorry for him when he was being so melodramatic. Actually, it was hard to feel sorry for Rick, period. "Tell me what happened."

"Larry from up the street called me this morning. He always goes to work early, you know."

"I know. Get to the part about Ginger."

"When Larry tried to back out of his driveway he couldn't because her car was parked in the street, blocking him. It was just sitting there, not moving." He paused, gulped and blinked a couple of times. His eyes were a little damp. Maybe he truly was upset. It's hard to see the genuine emotion when there's so much phoniness surrounding it. "She was in the car. Dead." His voice choked on the last word. Real or pretend choking? I'd put money on the *pretend* choice.

"So Larry called you?"

Rick nodded. "He knows her—knew her, knew she used to live with me, and he knew we broke up. He figured she had too much to drink, came to confront me and passed out in her car."

"She came to confront you but parked two houses up from your place?"

"She was probably watching my house to see when Robin left so she could talk to me alone."

Translation: *She was stalking him to see if the new woman would come out so she could make a scene.*

"Okay, Larry called you this morning and you went out to wake Ginger up?"

He bit his lip and nodded. "Do you have some place we can sit down?"

I pointed toward the door to the small office. "We have a couple of chairs in there."

"Thank you." He smiled weakly. "Can I have a glass of water?"

Oh, good grief! "Of course. Have a seat and I'll bring it to you."

I got him a glass of tap water, a compromise between refusing him anything and giving him bottled water.

I grabbed a cold can of Coke for myself and went to the office where he sat with his elbows on the desk and his head in his hands. Maybe I was being too hard on him. Surely even Rick had some genuine emotions. He must have cared for Ginger. He lived with her for several months, and he did look a mess.

I set the glass of water on the desk and laid a hand on his shoulder. "I'm sorry about Ginger."

He looked up, his expression tormented. Or a good imitation thereof. "Have you ever seen a dead person?"

"Well, yeah. Remember when you were trying to convince me to sell my house to that guy, and he dropped dead on the sidewalk out front?"

"That's different. He was a stranger. Ginger was somebody I knew, somebody I once loved." Naturally his dead body trauma was worse than mine. "Not as much as I loved you, of course."

"Don't start with that." I moved my chair as far away from him as I could get in the small office and popped open my Coke. Talking to Rick is always a two-Coke or three-glasses-of-wine deal. "Tell me how she died."

He shook his head, took a drink of the water and made a face. "This is terrible. Don't you have bottled water?"

"Sold out." Yes, it was a lie, but the idea of fetching purified water for such an unpurified person seemed wrong. "How did Ginger die? Knife wounds? Gun shot? Poison?"

"Her head was smashed. There was blood in her hair and all over the car. It was terrible." He shuddered and rubbed his eyes again.

Another person murdered in the same way Bob was killed. Maybe that would get the cops' attention. Maybe the murders were linked and that would force them to make every effort to find Bob's killer.

Yeah, and maybe JFK's assassination was connected to Lincoln's.

Ginger and Bob had absolutely nothing in common. My fleeting moment of optimism vanished as quickly as it came.

"I doubt she smashed her own head in, so I think suicide is out."

Rick took another drink of the tap water. "I don't know any of the details. Your *boyfriend*—" he spat out the word— "wouldn't tell me anything."

Made sense that Trent would have been there. He was a homicide detective on the small local police force. Pleasant Grove doesn't have a lot of homicides or a lot of homicide detectives.

"Deal with it," I said. "If you're here because you think Trent might have told me more than he told you, he didn't and he won't." In the shadows of the night Trent and I talked of our lives and hopes and dreams. He told me his deepest fears and his innermost needs. But he wouldn't tell me squat about an *ongoing investigation*.

Rick scowled. "That's not why I'm here. I'm here because...because I needed to talk to somebody." He leaned forward and grabbed my hand before I could yank it away. He has quick reflexes.

I twisted my hand out of his grip. "You don't think it's a little weird to go to your ex-wife for comfort when your ex-lover is murdered?"

"You knew her too."

"Not really. I met her a couple of times, and she made a scene on my front porch night before last." I rose. Surely I'd been compassionate long enough to satisfy whatever rules of compassion existed for ex-husbands. "I'm so sorry for your loss. I really need to get back to work. I can't leave Paula with all the cleanup."

He stood. "Can I call you later?"

"Sure." Promise him anything to get rid of him then don't answer the phone.

We walked through the restaurant together. The tables were empty. Brandon still sat at the counter and Paula stood behind it.

Rick paused at the front door and turned to give me another bone-crushing hug. I grimaced, patted his back and shoved him away.

He smiled sadly and squeezed my hand. "Thank you for being there, Lindsay. It means a lot to me. You mean a lot to me. I'll call you later."

He walked out the door then turned back to smile and wave. Oh, gag.

I spun away, back to the restaurant. Brandon and Paula watched me with expressions of concern.

"My ex," I explained to Brandon. "He's...um...well, there are a lot of reasons he's my ex, and you just saw a few of them."

Brandon slid off his stool and came toward me. "Are you okay?"

"I'm fine. He's annoying but harmless."

Brandon put a tentative hand on my shoulder. "Are you sure? He seemed pretty aggressive."

"He is, but not in that way. Rick's a salesman with Rheims Commercial Real Estate, very successful, which means very pushy."

"What did he mean about somebody being murdered?"

"He found his ex-girlfriend's body this morning. She was parked up the street from his house."

He grimaced. "No wonder he was so upset." He slid a card from his shirt pocket and handed it to me. "I wrote my cell number on the back. If he gives you any more trouble, call me."

I accepted the card. "Thank you. That's very sweet, but I'll be fine. Rick Kramer has been a huge thorn in my side for a lot of years, but the worst he's done is give me gray hairs and drive me to drink. Speaking of that, I think I'll have another Coke."

"Promise you'll call me if you need me."

"Okay."

He smiled and left. He didn't know about the code word.

Paula locked the door behind him. "Things are never dull around here, but I do believe that's the first time I've seen somebody go all protective over you."

I shrugged. "It was nice of him to offer, but I can take care of myself."

"As I recall, Fred and Trent have stepped in a couple of times to save your neck."

"I would have been fine even if they hadn't showed up."

Paula looked at me.

I looked at her.

That statement was so ludicrous, we both burst into laughter.

We cleaned and locked up. As we headed for our cars, I couldn't stop my gaze from going to the outline that marked the place where Bob had died.

The spots of blood were brown now, but I knew what they were. The lifeblood of a person.

Maybe I'd been too hard on Rick. It was devastating when someone you knew and cared about was murdered. I had to blink back tears when I looked at the evidence of Bob's murder and I hadn't seen the body. Rick had actually found Ginger's body. Maybe I'd answer when he called and be compassionate some more.

Or maybe not.

I got in my car and took out my cell phone to call Trent so he wouldn't call me when Fred and I were talking to Peterson. He gets a little upset when I *interfere* (his word, not mine) in *ongoing investigations*. Besides, he just loves it when I call him while I'm driving.

I put my Bluetooth in my ear, dialed his cell number and drove down the alley to the street.

He answered on the second ring. "Hi, gorgeous."

"Hey, sexy. I hear you met with my ex this morning. How fun was that?" I turned into traffic and prepared to be angry at the other drivers. If everybody would just forget those stupid speed restrictions, we'd all get to our destinations faster and my blood pressure would be a lot lower.

"Talking to Rick is almost as much fun as a root canal without Novocain," Trent said. "He must have called you about Ginger."

"He called me a couple of times but I refused to talk to him so he came by and made a scene. Selling real estate and making scenes are his major talents."

Some jerk pulled directly in front of me from a side street. I started to honk but Trent would have heard the sound and realized I was driving and talking. He doesn't think I can multi-task. I settled for glaring at the man. He couldn't see my expression, but it made me feel better.

"What did he tell you about Ginger?" Trent asked.

"That he found her parked up the street from his house with her head bashed in. He said you refused to tell him anything."

Trent laughed. "I kind of enjoyed not telling him anything. It's pretty easy to push his buttons."

"For once, I'm good with you not telling me anything about the crime. I didn't really like her, I don't want to talk about her, and I don't care who killed her." That last comment wasn't true, but I thought maybe he'd tell me more if he thought I wasn't interested.

"Actually, I can tell you something about her murder."

It worked!

I braked at a four-way stop sign. The car already sitting at the cross street didn't move. Great. Had to be someone who was busy texting or someone who thought it was polite to let the woman go first even though it totally messed up the timing. In the first instance I could start through about the time he looked up from his cell phone and end up with a dent in my passenger door. In the second instance, we could be there all day if I didn't take the initiative.

Oh, well, what was one more dent? I barreled through the intersection without incident.

"Okay, what can you tell me about Ginger's murder?"

"Ginger's GPS shows she drove to your house last night and the night before. You need to come to the station. You're a person of interest."

Chapter Seven

I suppose being a person of interest is better than being a person of boredom. However, when I walked into the Pleasant Grove Police Department as a person of interest in my ex-husband's ex-girlfriend's murder, I would have much preferred to be the boring kind.

Detective Adam Trent—not Trent, the man I'd spent the weekend with—met me at the front desk in his usual uniform...rumpled sports coat, rumpled slacks and rumpled hair. His hazel eyes showed little trace of green. He was not happy. Neither was I.

"Thanks for coming in, Lindsay." I was surprised he didn't call me *Miss Powell*. "Detective Lawson is going to take your statement." He turned and headed through the door, leading me to an empty interrogation room.

I'd actually been in that room once before when we thought Rick was dead. Should have known he wasn't. Rick is like one of those monsters in the horror movies who keep coming no matter how many times the heroine shoots him. Not that I've ever shot Rick. Thought about it, planned it, but never actually done it.

"Go on in," Trent said. "Detective Lawson will be right with you."

He gave me a brief pat on the fanny before walking away. That pat came from boyfriend Trent, not Detective Adam Trent. He was still in there somewhere.

I sat in one of the wooden chairs at the wooden table. If the purpose of that room was to make people so uncomfortable they'd confess to anything just to get out of there, it was serving its purpose.

Gerald Lawson entered with a regular size notepad. "Afternoon, Lindsay. How are you?"

"There are blood spots in the alley behind my business from my friend's murder, my ex-husband just showed up at my restaurant and acted like a crazy man, and now you all have hauled me in for questioning. How do you think I am?"

The detective folded his long body into a chair across from me and set his notepad on the table. "I'm sorry you're having a bad day. We won't keep you long."

Lawson is a nice guy. He's just not into emotion. Except for the fact that he has gray hair, he reminds me of Sergeant Joe Friday on that old show, *Dragnet*. *Just the facts, ma'am*.

That day he lived up to Joe Friday's image and to my nickname for him, Granite Man. His thin lips formed a straight line, and his narrow, chiseled features showed no sign of any expression. However, I suppose that in itself is an expression...and not a friendly one.

"How well did you know Virginia Lancaster?"

"Who?" I shook my head. "I don't know her. Good grief, has somebody else been murdered?"

Lawson took a photograph from his folder and laid it on the table in front of me.

I looked at the picture. "Oh. That's Ginger. Virginia Lancaster? I didn't know her real name. Obviously I didn't know her very well if I didn't even know her real name."

"She came to your house twice over the last forty-eight hours. You knew her well enough for her to visit in the middle of the night."

I leaned forward and spread my hands on the table. "Hey, it's not like I sent her an invitation to visit. I can't be responsible for every nut job my ex-husband sleeps with."

I waited for a response, an apology or something. Of course I got none. He stared at me and waited. I'd seen this on TV. The cop sits quietly while the suspect spills his—or her—guts. I just sat there and stared back at him. Two could play that game.

"Okay," I finally admitted, "she came to my house night before last to yell at me." I'm not very good at sitting still and being silent. I'm a lot better at spilling my guts.

"About what?"

"She wanted me to let her have Rick."

Lawson looked even stonier. "Are you back together with your ex-husband?"

"Of course not! You know that Trent and I...well, we...uh..." I waved a hand to indicate words I wasn't sure I should be saying in an interrogation room where the conversation was probably being recorded. It would not likely be a good idea for a suspect—excuse me, person of interest—to say she and another detective were lovers.

Lawson raised one eyebrow ever so slightly, maybe two centimeters, but said nothing.

"Come on! You know better than that. Rick told her we were getting back together because he has somebody new and didn't have the courage to be honest."

"What did you tell her?"

Yay! I made him talk even though I had to spill my guts twice. "I told her she could have Rick, that I'd give him up, he was all hers."

"If you aren't back with your ex, how could you give him up?"

I heaved a deep sigh of frustration at Lawson's inability to understand how things worked in the real world. "I just said that to shut her up. What would you have done if some crazy woman showed up on your porch in the middle of the night, shouting at you?"

"You could have called the police."

"Why would I do that? She wasn't waving a gun or threatening me. She was just drunk and pitiful. It was easier to say, *yeah, okay, whatever you want*, and then she went away."

"Why did she come back last night?"

I heaved another deep sigh to show my annoyance. "Since I didn't talk to her, I have no idea. Maybe she came to see somebody else in my neighborhood."

"Who?"

"How would I know? She didn't put an update on her Facebook page."

"Are you friends on Facebook?"

This was getting ridiculous. "I don't have a Facebook page. It was a joke."

"When did you last see Ms. Lancaster?"

"I told you already. Night before last when she came to my door."

"What time was that?"

"It was maybe a half hour after you and Trent left. Check it out. I'm sure you keep better records of your time than I do of mine." I slid my chair back. "Are we finished?"

"How would you categorize your relationship with Ms. Lancaster?"

I clenched my fists, gritted my teeth and reminded myself that this man was Trent's partner and friend, that he'd hugged me when he thought Rick was dead, that he was only doing his job and wasn't deliberately trying to irritate me.

"Nonexistent. I saw Ginger a couple of times with Rick, and then she came to my house in the middle of the night and carried on like a drunken banshee. We were not BFFs. We didn't do lunch or exchange friendship bracelets. I didn't even know her real name until you told me a few minutes ago."

"Who would want to harm Ms. Lancaster?"

I stood, placed both hands on the table and leaned toward him. "Funniest thing, she hasn't confided in me lately. The only person I know who'd have reason to kill her is her former lover, Rick." Yes, I threw him under the bus and gleefully anticipated the way he'd squish when the wheels rolled over him. "She was killed while sitting in her car up the street from his house. Obviously she was spying on him, probably planning to make a big scene with the new girlfriend. Maybe Rick killed her so she couldn't. Maybe she already made a big scene and the girlfriend killed her."

"Do you have a name for the new girlfriend?"

With one foot, I shoved my chair back. It hit the wall with a satisfying thud. "I think he called her Robin. You're the cops. It's your job to find out that kind of stuff."

He slid the picture into his folder and stood. "That's all for now. Thank you for coming in."

I started toward the door.

"Did you bring any cookies with you?"

I could not freaking believe he would grill me as if I were a murder suspect and then ask for chocolate! I opened my mouth to tell him exactly what I thought then closed it. Over the years I've learned that it is never a good idea to rag on a cop when that cop stops me and accuses me of exceeding some arbitrary speed limit. Very likely the same thing applied to a cop accusing me of killing somebody.

I smiled at Lawson. "I'm sorry. I didn't bring anything today—short notice. But I promise I will tomorrow."

He nodded. "I really like your chocolate chip cookies."

"I'll bring you a dozen with nuts."

His lips twitched slightly. He almost smiled.

I left the room and started down the hall toward the exit.

Trent came up behind me. "You okay?"

"I'm fine," I snapped.

"Want me to come over for a while tonight?"

Yes, yes, yes! "No." I walked stiffly through the reception area and out the front door.

Trent followed me and put a hand on my shoulder. "I get the idea you're upset."

I turned to face him. "Who's asking? My boyfriend Trent or Detective Adam Trent of the Pleasant Grove Police Department?"

He grinned, a wide, open expression that always makes me want to grin back. "Both of us."

I refused to grin back. I scowled instead. "I'm not ready to be charmed. I'm angry at you for treating me like a suspect. You know I'd never kill anybody."

"Of course I know that. But we have to follow procedure. We have to check out everybody associated with the victim."

"Then go check out Rick. He just loves talking to you."

"Rick and his lawyer are coming in tomorrow."

"Already lawyered up? That tells you something!"

"Do you think Rick killed Ginger?"

I didn't, but I'd been wrong about Rick before, like when I thought he was a nice man and married him. "It's possible."

I stalked down the steps, away from Trent and Detective Adam Trent.

"I'll call you tonight."

"Maybe by then I'll be over being mad and answer the phone." I didn't stop, just threw the words over my shoulder. "And maybe I won't and I won't."

I drove home without incident or ticket and fed Henry.

Fred called. "Are you ready?" he asked by way of greeting.

"Of course." My answer was automatic, but it took me a moment to figure out what I was supposed to be ready for. In the course of being a person of interest, I'd forgotten about the proposed visit to Peterson.

"What are you wearing?" he asked.

I looked at my blue jeans and red knit shirt, both with traces of chocolate on them. "Black suit," I lied.

"Good. Come on over." He hung up.

I raced upstairs and changed into my trusty black suit, the one I only wear to funerals, visits to mobsters and other excursions with Fred. That suit is getting a little worn, and I haven't been to a funeral in a long time.

Henry accompanied me to Fred's then left to pursue his own agenda. I fervently hoped I would return home to an empty porch—no mice, no flowers, no bottles of wine. After Ginger's demise, I assumed Rick's offerings would cease, but Henry's would likely continue. With all the little critters scurrying around, busily preparing for winter, he might even double up.

Fred, wearing a dark suit and tie, opened the door and stepped out. "Why did you arrive home so late?"

Further evidence he didn't know *everything*. I wasn't sure if I was elated or disappointed. "Cops."

"Lindsay, whether you think those speed limits are valid or not, they're going to give you a ticket when you exceed them."

"Only when they catch me." I followed him to the driveway where his vintage white Mercedes waited. If I kept my Celica a few more years, would it change from *old* to *vintage*? "Anyway, that's not what they hauled me in for. They think I killed Ginger."

He halted, his hand on the passenger door. "Ginger's dead? They think you killed her?"

"Yes and yes. I'm shocked you didn't know all that."

He opened the door and I slid onto the soft leather seat.

"I've been busy today," he said.

"With Sophie?"

He closed my door, walked around to the driver's side, and got in. "We're going to visit A-Plus Construction. There may be more to Bob's death than I first thought."

"You found out something about Nick Peterson, didn't you?"

He eased the car from the driveway onto the street. I have no idea why he rigidly adheres to the speed limit. I've been with him when he drove like Jeff Gordon, and with his hacking skills, he could get out of any tickets.

"Maybe," he said in response to my question. "His real name is Nicholas Peretti. Remember my friend, Donato Orsini?"

"Like I could ever forget meeting a mobster and you telling the man he shouldn't be smoking in his own office! I thought we'd both soon be wearing concrete shoes at the bottom of the Missouri River."

"Donato's finally decided to quit smoking. I was forced to get his wife involved."

"So you snitched off the mob guy to his wife? Why not just tell on him to his mother?"

He moved onto the freeway, driving at precisely the speed limit. "His mother's not in the best of health. I didn't want to worry her."

"Of course you didn't. So getting back to Nick Peterson-Peretti, what did you find out about him?"

"He and Donato go back a long way."

"You mean Nick's a member of the mob? You think he had Bob killed? Why would he offer him a job and then put out a hit on him?"

Fred proceeded calmly down the highway as if I wasn't freaking out in the seat next to him. "Donato said Nick's a straight-up guy and has been out of that world for several years. Nevertheless, he may know something. It's quite a coincidence that Bob was killed right after he accepted a job with Nick."

"Wow, that sounds familiar! Oh, yeah, I said it last night."

"On the other hand, coincidences do happen or we wouldn't have a word for them."

I was already in a bad mood with Trent, and Fred's ambivalent attitude wasn't helping my disposition. However, we were on our way to talk to Nick Peterson-Peretti, a meeting I'd pushed for, so I refrained from expressing my irritation.

We drove to a warehouse type building north of the city. The structure was one story and ordinary in design but neat and sturdy. A few large pieces of equipment dotted the parking lot with lots of empty space in between. I assumed the machines that usually occupied the empty slots were off somewhere digging basements and building houses.

Fred parked close to the front door and we got out.

"Who are we?" I asked as we approached the door.

"You're Lindsay Powell and I'm Fred Sommers." He shook his head. "Sometimes I worry about you, Lindsay. Have you been snorting Henry's catnip?"

"I meant—"

Fred swung the door open.

I stopped talking.

The receptionist looked up from her crossword puzzle.

Fred handed her a card. "Fred Sommers and Lindsay Powell to see Nick Peterson."

It would have been nice if he'd let me see that card before we walked in. We might be Fred Sommers and Lindsay Powell, but I was pretty sure we weren't entering Nick Peterson's office as a chocolatier and her strange neighbor.

The receptionist advised her boss of our presence. A moment later a tall, thin man in khakis and a white cotton shirt with rolled-up sleeves strode through the door at the side of the room. Steel gray at his temples emphasized the blackness of hair combed straight back from his forehead. A huge smile brightened his tan face. He grabbed my hand in one of his, and moisture shone in his dark eyes. "I'm glad to get to meet you, Lindsay. Bob told me all about what you did for him."

I was speechless. We really were there as a chocolatier and her strange neighbor.

He turned to Fred and gave him an enthusiastic handshake. "And you must be Fred. Come in, come in." He released Fred's hand and waved toward the open door. "Leslie, would you get us three coffees? Cream? Sugar?"

Fred flinched. He's very finicky about his coffee. Grinds his own beans. He may grow them for all I know. "Black for me." The fact he didn't refuse the coffee told me he was more concerned about sucking up to Nick Peretti than about guarding his taste buds.

I lifted a hand and shook my head. "Thank you, none for me." I'd accepted coffee in Donato Orsino's office and even tried to drink it because I was intimidated. I was not going to do that again. Fred would have to suck up enough for both of us.

"Soda? Tea?"

"Do you have Coke?"

"Sure. Leslie, please bring us two black coffees and a Coke."

We followed Nick into his office. It was like the exterior of the building...sturdy, practical, no frills. A large metal desk covered with papers dominated the room, and a large window looked out onto the parking lot. Not a great view, but perhaps looking at his machines was a great view for him.

Nick sat behind the desk and motioned Fred and me to a couple of brown vinyl chairs. He leaned forward and folded his hands on the desktop. His smile faded. "So what's going on with Bob? His death wasn't just some scumbag wanting to rob him, was it?"

"No," I said.

"We're not sure." Fred just had to disagree with me.

Leslie entered the room with a tray holding two brown mugs and one beautiful red can. She set one mug in front of Fred, the other in front of Nick, and I took the red can. Just the way I like it...cold and straight, no ice diluting the bold, sparkling flavor.

Leslie left, closing the door behind her. Fred took a sip of his coffee, grimaced slightly, and set the cup back on the desk. I took a long pull on my Coke. Nothing like being grilled by the cops to work up a thirst.

"Who do you think killed Bob?" Nick asked.

"We were hoping you could help us figure it out. My friend, Donato Orsini, said you might be able to give us some information about Bob's past associates."

Nick's smile returned. "You must be the Fred who blabbed to Donato's wife about his smoking. She nagged him until he agreed to stop."

"I am."

Nick picked up his coffee, sat back and laughed. "You got balls. That woman's a holy terror."

"Marie and I go way back."

Nick nodded. "Yep, yep. I knew her before they got married. Me and Donato go way back too. Had some interesting times."

"How about Bob? Did he run with the same crowd?"

Nick shook his head. "Not like you mean. Bob was…" He looked around the room as if searching for hidden microphones. If they were hidden, he wasn't likely to find them. "Bob was a straight arrow. Him and me, we started out in the construction business about the same time." He held up a hand as if to restrain whatever we were going to say. "You may think that meant we were rivals, but we weren't. Bob started a few months before me, and we met at one of those industry get-togethers. Bob helped me with a lot of my startup things. I had different…" He paused and looked from one to the other of us. "I had different assets. You know what I mean? So I was able to help him too."

Fred looked completely comfortable in the uncomfortable vinyl chair. He sat with his hands folded in his lap, listening to the almost-confession about possibly dubious business practices as if Peterson was discussing a couple of boys with lemonade stands. "So the two of you pooled your resources and each of you developed a successful company," he said.

"Exactly. Business was good, life was good. And then Linda got sick. They grew up next door to each other, got married right out of high school. Her death hit Bob pretty hard."

"So hard he lost his company?" Fred asked.

Nick nodded. "He couldn't get by without her. He stayed away from work a lot when she was sick, then after she died, he just didn't seem to care. Didn't have the will to work or to live. He disappeared, went away from all of us. Tell you the truth, until he showed up here last week looking for a job, I thought he was dead."

"And now he is," I said. "As soon as he reappeared, somebody killed him. Does that seem to you to be a pretty big coincidence?"

"Yeah, it does. I've thought about that over and over, tried to figure out who could have wanted Bob dead."

Fred didn't speak. Neither did I. We both knew about the method the cops used to get suspects to talk. It had worked quite well on me.

Nick looked down at his desk. "Bob was a good guy, but we all make mistakes, do things we wish we hadn't done." He lifted his head and looked directly at Fred then at me. "He loved Linda. But they went through a rough patch."

I was pretty sure I didn't want to hear any more about Bob's rough patch. I wanted to continue to think of him as a good man who deserved a second chance. I took a big drink of my Coke and wished for a five-pound slab of chocolate.

Nick's eyes narrowed. "Bob was a good guy," he repeated. "Him and Linda both wanted kids, but that just didn't happen. I guess they blamed each other for a while. Then Tina came along. She was Bob's bookkeeper, and the two of them spent some long hours together on the job." He shrugged.

"So Bob cheated on his wife?" *The woman whose death had been so painful, it caused his downward spiral?* Maybe he hadn't deserved those extra cookies I gave him. I knew only too well what it felt like to be married to a cheater. Not a pleasant feeling.

Would Trent ever cheat on me? With the hours he worked, he didn't have time.

Besides, he just wouldn't. He played by the rules, colored inside the lines. He was too honest. Apparently Bob hadn't been.

"The affair didn't mean anything," Nick continued, "and it didn't last long. When Linda came down with the cancer, he broke it off with Tina. The whole time Linda fought cancer, Bob was right there by her side, and it just about killed him when she died. She was his wife, his soul mate. He didn't want to live without her, and he blamed himself. He thought the cancer was his punishment for cheating. That's when he started drinking, quit caring and lost everything."

Maybe he really did regret what he'd done. As Nick said, we all make mistakes. Whatever Bob had done, he didn't deserve to be murdered.

"I helped him make a comeback so he could be killed." I didn't realize I'd spoken the words aloud until Nick scowled.

"No," he protested. "If he hadn't quit drinking, he'd have been dead in a few months from the booze.

You made him feel like he mattered, like he wasn't worthless. He was getting back to his old self. He told me he had hope for the first time in a lot of years."

"You think this Tina could have killed him?" I asked.

Nick shook his head. "Tina got upset when Bob dumped her, but she's not violent, and she's a little bitty thing, barely five feet. Bob was tall. No way she could have hit him over the head like that." He tapped a finger on his desk several times and looked into the distance as if undecided about something. Finally his gaze returned to us. "But Ken, her husband—"

"Husband? She was married too?" The story was becoming more sordid by the moment. *Jerry Springer*, here we come.

"Still is married. Kenneth Wilson. He works for me. Worked for me then. Him and Tina weren't getting along, and she was talking about leaving. Ken's a good worker, but he didn't treat Tina right. He's pretty hot-tempered. When Bob needed a good bookkeeper, I told Tina about the job. Thought it would be a good deal for both of them. Bob would have a top-notch employee and Tina could get away from Ken."

"But she didn't?" I asked.

Peterson shook his head. "Linda got sick and Bob broke it off with Tina. She went back to Ken, and they had a baby. Got three of them now. I guess she feels pretty trapped."

"But you let this Ken keep working for you?" I sounded aghast. I was aghast.

Fred and Peterson both looked at me as if I were slightly nuts.

"He's a good worker," Peterson repeated. "They're hard to come by. He does his job, never causes any problems at work. I wouldn't know about his home life if Tina hadn't told my wife."

So abusing his wife is okay as long as he doesn't bring it to work? I bit my tongue and refrained from speaking since we were trying to get information out of Peterson. Reprimanding him for questionable morals wasn't likely to help.

"Did he know Bob was coming to work for you?" Fred asked. He hadn't moved from his relaxed posture, but I could tell he was no longer relaxed. Nothing physical, more like an aura. A hunting dog on point without actually pointing.

"Yeah. I told him. My company's pretty good size. There wasn't any reason he and Bob would ever have to see each other. Ken gave me some grief about it, but I told him Bob had paid for what he did."

"So Ken knew about the affair?"

Nick grimaced. "Yeah. Bob confessed when the doctor told him Linda was dying. He thought if he admitted to what he'd done and asked for forgiveness, God would let Linda live."

"Bargaining with God is a fairly common thing when somebody we love is dying." Fred sounded as if he knew what he was talking about. Was this a clue to his past? Had somebody he loved died? Had he loved somebody?

I made a mental note to ask later. Not that I expected an answer. He even refused to answer when I asked him if he had a mother or came from a test tube.

"Did the police talk to Ken?" Fred asked.

"Hell, no. I didn't tell the cops any of the story I just told you. I wouldn't be telling you except you all are friends with Donato so you're like a member of the family."

Oh, good, I was included as a member of another dysfunctional family. Like my own wasn't enough.

"Can we talk to Ken?" Fred asked. "Is he on a job site today?"

Nick drummed his fingers on the desktop—four of them this time—as he studied Fred and then me. Finally he picked up a pencil, wrote something on a piece of paper, and handed it to Fred. "This is his home address. Yesterday he asked me what the cops wanted and today he called in sick."

Chapter Eight

Fred actually exceeded the speed limit by four miles an hour as we drove to Kenneth Wilson's house.

"What was in that coffee?" I asked.

"Used motor oil, I believe. Why? Did you want to get a copy of the recipe for your shop?"

"I just wondered if it was spiked with meth or something. You're driving over the speed limit. That's not like you."

"I want to get there before dark."

The sun was sinking closer to the horizon as we zipped (speaking relatively) along the freeway. "Don't tell me you're scared to confront that man after dark."

"If he runs, he'll be easier to find in the daylight. Of course, he's had twenty-four hours. He may be miles from here already." He exited the freeway and turned onto a residential street.

"If he's on the lam, we'll hunt him down, right?"

"Of course."

I wasn't sure if Fred's determination to catch Bob's killer came from a need to find justice in an often unjust world or from his OCD nature, unwilling to rest until all ends were tidied up. Probably the latter.

I was still determined to find him for Bob's sake. Yes, I'd just discovered the man wasn't perfect, but he'd taken some hard knocks and was making an effort to rebuild his life. If Ken had killed him just because he didn't want to have to work with his wife's former lover—well, that certainly gave him the motive, but not the right. As often as I'd contemplated murdering Rick, I'd never thought about killing any of his bimbos. But I'd never been forced to work with them. That might have made a difference.

Fred pulled over to the curb in front of a mundane house in a mundane suburban neighborhood. It was the sort of area where both parents worked and left the kids at day care during the week then got together with the neighbors on weekends, barbecued hamburgers and drank beer. Kids were riding their bicycles along the sidewalk, and a guy two houses down was watering his lawn. Wholesome. Just the kind of neighborhood where a killer would live.

I opened my car door and stepped out. Fred took something from a canvas bag in the back seat and put it in his inside jacket pocket. Gun? Shiv? Blackjack?

He got out of the car and closed his door.

"What did you just put in your pocket?" I asked as we started up the walk toward the house with gray siding and closed curtains.

"Something I may need."

"Well, duh. I didn't think you were taking an empty soda can with you." Though Fred might be able to find a use for that.

He didn't respond, just kept walking. I don't claim to be psychic, but that ordinary house seemed to radiate evil. I edged a bit closer to Fred.

"Got it under control." That's about as close as he comes to offering comfort.

We climbed the three steps to the front porch that was so small it barely qualified as such. Another thing I like about old houses. They have big porches.

Fred pushed the doorbell. It worked. I could hear the raucous sound through the door.

We waited.

No one came to the door.

Fred rang the bell again then knocked forcefully. "Open up! Immigration!"

"They're not immigrants," I whispered.

"Exactly. So they'll open the door to tell me I have the wrong house." He banged loudly again. "Don't make me break down this door!"

"I think maybe it's illegal to impersonate an immigration officer."

"I'm not impersonating an immigration officer. I simply spoke the word 'immigration.' I can't help what inference people take from that."

I liked that logic. I was learning a lot from Fred.

The door swung open and a woman holding an ice bag to her face gazed at us from one eye. The other was swollen almost shut. Since she was short, slim and female, I assumed this was Tina.

Fred flashed some sort of badge. He did it so rapidly the woman couldn't possibly have seen what it was. Neither could I. Police? CIA? FBI? Termite Inspector?

"I need to speak with Kenneth Wilson."

The woman lifted her bruised chin. "Have you got a search warrant?"

She knew how this game was played. I wondered how Fred was going to deal with that request.

"I don't need a search warrant." He sounded confident and tough.

Her good eye widened.

A door slammed somewhere in the house.

"Excuse me." Fred leapt from the porch and ran around the house toward the back yard. Apparently our suspect was on the lam.

Tina started to close the door but I grabbed it. "Did Kenneth do that to you?"

I expected her to deny it, try to convince me she'd run into a door or fallen down the stairs even though the house had only one story.

"What if he did?" she asked. "It's none of your concern."

True, but that had never stopped me before. "You don't have to take that. You can leave him."

"Lady, you need to mind your own business." She tried again to close the door, but I was stronger.

"I was Bob's friend. Do you think he'd want you to tolerate this kind of treatment?"

Her grip on the door loosened and she became very still. I wasn't sure if she was going to cry in grief or scream in anger.

"Bob's dead." The two lifeless words fell from her lips, making me feel her pain more surely than if she'd cried or screamed.

"I know he is, and there's a good chance your husband killed him."

She stared at me in silence. Her expression didn't change. Either she'd already considered that possibility and dismissed it or she knew for a fact that Kenneth had killed her former lover.

"Are you going to let him get away with it?" I asked.

"He said he didn't do it."

They'd talked about it. "Does he always tell the truth?"

She laughed, a brief burst of hollow sound. Her open eye focused to the left of my face, refusing to look me in the eye. "Ken's a good man. This hasn't happened in a long time." She bit her lip and returned her gaze to mine. "I've got three kids, and he takes care of all of us."

"As he should."

"Well, two of them. But my oldest is Bob's son."

"Oh." Add another layer of motive.

"You knew Bob?" she asked.

I nodded. "He came to my restaurant, Death by Chocolate." No need to specify the exact location he came to—the trash bin behind the restaurant. "We talked. We became friends."

"He told you about me?"

I considered the question. In a way he kind of, sort of, had told me. By telling me Nick was hiring him, he'd led me to Nick who had told me. If I wanted to get information from this woman, there could be only one answer. "Yes."

"I loved him."

"He cared for you." Okay, that might have been an outright lie, but it might have been the truth. Surely he wouldn't have had a relationship with her if he hadn't cared for her.

Her swollen lips twitched into something resembling a smile. "I know. He cared for me, but he didn't love me. He loved his wife."

"Did you still love him after he confessed everything to your husband?"

She flinched. "I was angry with him for a long time. But I guess in the long run the truth is always better than lies."

"Does Ken feel the same way about the truth thing?"

"Ken's got a temper."

Laughter sounded from the side yard, and I turned. Fred, immaculate in his black suit, white shirt and burgundy tie, came across the grass with one arm wrapped around the neck of a burly guy wearing a wife-beater T-shirt and stained blue jeans. Ken, I presumed. To my surprise, Fred wasn't choking him. They seemed to be best buds.

"Lindsay, we've got the wrong house, but look who I found! We both went to the same high school!"

I doubted it.

"Come on in," the man invited. "Let's have a drink to the Bulldogs!"

They brushed past us into the house.

Judging from the sound of Ken's voice and the smell of his breath, he had been drinking to the Bulldogs for quite a while.

Tina gave me a confused look. I shrugged. Odds were Ken was did not have an aged bottle of Cabernet Sauvignon open and breathing, so Fred probably wasn't doing this because he wanted to drink with the man. Doubtless he had a plan, but he hadn't confided in me.

"Tina! Bring us a couple of beers," Ken shouted from somewhere inside the house.

"If he's too drunk or lazy to get them himself, he doesn't need them," I said.

Tina went inside.

I followed right behind her. From the living room I could see Fred and Ken seated at the kitchen table. "I was married to a jerk once," I said quietly. "You don't have to take this. We can have a confrontation right now with Fred and me to help you."

She stopped halfway through the living room and turned back to me. "And then you'll go home and my kids and I will be here alone with him."

"Where are your kids?"

"At my sister's house until this blows over. Ken's been drinking ever since he heard about Bob." She continued through the kitchen door.

"About time!" Ken called.

She went straight to the refrigerator, took out two beers, popped them open and set them in front of Fred and Ken.

Fred wrapped his fingers around his can. "Thank you."

Ken did not follow his polite example. Without comment he lifted the can to his lips. I had to resist the urge to shove that can up his nose.

Without waiting for an invitation…which wasn't likely to come…I slid back a chair and sat down between the two men then scooted my chair as far away from Ken as possible.

Fear spread over Tina's face as her gaze settled on Ken. I hoped he'd do something violent to protest my sitting at his table uninvited. I was looking forward to Fred taking him down. When he got him on the floor, I'd help by kicking him a few times.

"This your woman?" Ken asked.

I supposed it was a natural assumption since I was practically sitting in Fred's lap in my effort to put distance between Ken and me.

"This is Lindsay," Fred answered.

"Honey, get Fred's woman a beer."

"No, thank you."

"Soda pop?"

"No, thank you." I would have liked a Coke but I wasn't going to accept anything from that creature.

Ken clutched his beer and pointed at Fred with one finger. "Hey, were you at that game a few years ago when our Bulldogs didn't let the other team score even a field goal?"

"Great game. That player—" Fred imitated Ken's gesture. "I can't think of his name. You know the one I'm talking about."

"Fields!"

"Yes! That's him. Amazing!"

Fred was really good with BS.

As they talked about the football team they supposedly had in common, Tina got another can of beer for Ken then slid timidly into a chair next to him.

Ken set down the empty can and grabbed the full one.

"You hear about that awful murder a couple of days ago?" Apparently Fred thought Ken had consumed enough alcohol that he could safely change the subject. "Happened in the alley behind the restaurant where a friend of mine works."

"No kidding? Right behind where your friend works?" Ken lifted his can for a big gulp.

"Yeah, some homeless guy got killed. What did the cops say his name was, Lindsay?"

"Bob. Bob Markham." I watched Ken's face closely.

I was not disappointed. His drunken camaraderie changed to anger. He glanced at Tina who sat rigidly in her chair. "Yeah, well, some people get what they deserve."

I bit my lip to keep from mouthing off.

Fred nodded. "Know what you mean. Some druggie living off decent people who work and pay taxes."

"Yeah, that's all he was. Just some old drunk living on the streets."

It did not escape my notice that Fred called Bob a *druggie* but Ken corrected it to *drunk*. He knew.

Fred lifted his beer to his lips, set it back on the table and nodded. "Beats me why the police are wasting so much time trying to find the killer. I mean, like you said, just some old drunk. He didn't leave a lot of clues, but they've got this technology they can use to detect the pattern of shoe treads up to twenty-four hours after the person walked through the alley."

Ken frowned. "Izzat right? How's that work? Wouldn't there be lots of shoe prints in that alley?"

"Not as many as you'd think. I hear they've nailed it down to one set of shoes." Fred clutched his beer and smiled. "Mind if I use your little boy's room? Stuff goes right through me. You know?"

I tensed. Fred had taken, at most, a couple of sips of his beer. He must be counting on Ken to be so drunk he wouldn't notice.

"Yeah, sure. Use the one in our bedroom. The one in the hall's a mess. Damn kids. Down the hall, last door on your right."

Fred rose, still holding his beer. "Thanks. Be right back. Lindsay, tell my buddy Ken all about thermography and how the cops can identify individual shoe prints and track down the exact pair of shoes that made them. She's better at this technical stuff than I am."

Fred piled one lie on top of another.

"Sure, thermography." I leaned forward, folded my hands on the table and cleared my throat, buying a few seconds to think of what to say. "Works on the principle of heat. Your body always produces heat."

Ken laughed raucously. "You know it, honey!"

I sat motionless for a moment, reminding myself that our visit had a purpose, and I should not mess up that purpose by reaching across the table and slapping that fool. "So you leave traces of your heat pattern everywhere you go. The cops can measure that heat pattern through the print of your shoes and go right to the pair of shoes that made the print." I was pretty impressed with my own BS.

Ken's brow furrowed in a scowl. "So you're saying if somebody's wearing a pair of Nikes just like thousands of other people, the cops can find that pair of shoes? How? They're all alike."

"No, they're not. Each pair of shoes has its own pattern, just like fingerprints and DNA. No two are exactly alike. All they have to do now is find the shoes worn by the guy who murdered Bob, compare them to the prints they have, and the guy's off to prison."

Did Ken go pale at that news? It was getting dark and nobody had turned on the light in the kitchen so I couldn't tell for sure.

He drained his beer and slammed the can down on the table. "They ought to give the guy a medal. Tina, get me another beer. Can't you see this one's empty? Get another one for my friend too."

"No, thanks." Fred appeared behind his chair and set an empty can on the table. I presumed he flushed the contents. "We've got to be going. Got to find that Russian immigrant." He held a hand across the table. "Sure nice to meet another Bulldog fan. Thank you much for the beer."

Ken shook his hand vigorously. "Let's go to the next game together."

Fred made a thumbs-up sign. "Deal. Call me. You've got my number."

Ken followed us to the door and slapped Fred on the back as we left. I didn't see Tina. I presumed she was still huddling in the kitchen. Maybe Ken would pass out on his way back through the living room. Maybe she'd then find the guts to grab one of her kids' baseball bats and beat him as severely as he'd beaten her.

That wasn't likely to happen.

We drove away from the ordinary house with all its extraordinary secrets. I was in a play in grade school and had to wear a bright orange tutu and an orange cardboard flower around my face. Getting away from Kenneth Wilson's house felt almost as good as getting off that stage.

"You gave that creep your phone number?" I asked.

"Of course not."

"You told him he had your number."

"I lied." He drove calmly down the street.

"About a lot of things. Thermography? Really? And then you left me to explain it?"

"I knew you could do it. If he tries to get rid of a pair of shoes, we'll know we've got the right guy." He turned a corner on all four wheels. Such a waste of a good engine.

"How will you know if he tries to get rid of a pair of shoes? Are you going to sit by his garbage can all night and watch him?"

"All I have to do is scan the video from the camera I put above the door in his bedroom."

"Is that what you got out of the bag and put in your pocket?" I turned around and looked at the back seat. Half a dozen canvas bags of various shapes and sizes remained. "What's in the rest of them?"

"Necessities. I applaud you for not going off on our suspect. I could feel your anger, and I don't blame you. But self control is essential when you're trying to get information."

"Or set somebody up."

"That too."

We rode in silence for a few moments. I hate to admit it, but there's something soothing about Fred's driving, sort of like a slow waltz down the street. I'd never tell him that, of course.

That night I wasn't soothed.

"I sure hope we get proof against Ken and can lock that jerk away for the rest of his life," I said. "I hate him because he killed my friend, and I hate him for what he's doing to Tina."

Fred's profile was a stern silhouette in the dark car. "The best we can do is hope to get him before..."

It's not like Fred to stop in the middle of a sentence, but I heard what he didn't say. *Before he kills Tina too.*

I learned nothing else during the remainder of our ride. I was tempted to reach into the back, pick up one of those canvas bags and open it. I didn't do it, but it gave me an idea.

I could plant a camera in Fred's house the way he'd done to Ken and see what he and Sophie were up to.

I burst into laughter at the ridiculous idea that I could get away with doing something like that.

"What's so funny?" he asked.

"You wouldn't understand."

We pulled into his driveway. "I'll see you safely inside your house then come back and put my car in the garage," he said.

"I live next door. I think I can make it on my own." I got out of the car and started across the yard. He walked beside me. "Seriously?" I asked. "Look. Henry's on my porch waiting. If anything was going on, he'd let me know."

"That's true, but you know I can't leave anything unfinished. I'm going with you."

As we got closer, I saw that Henry was holding something down with one big paw and ripping at it with his lion-sized teeth. I sighed. "Great. As long as you're here, you can dispose of Henry's gift."

"I don't think that's a mouse."

"Mouse, rabbit, bird, mole. I don't care what it is, I want it gone. One time he brought me a snake."

We reached the porch and Fred stooped to pick up the remnants of whatever Henry had brought home. Henry snarled. Of course he did. The gift was for me, not Fred.

"Fred will give it to me," I assured Henry.

"Lindsay, you need to see this."

"I'm pretty sure I don't."

"This gift is not from Henry."

Chapter Nine

From the shredded red wrapping paper and ribbon, Fred produced a small object that gleamed in the moonlight.

A crystal butterfly.

Rick knew how much I loved crystal, so sparkly with all those pretty rainbows. He gave me a crystal unicorn for our first anniversary. I still have it—not because it has sentimental value but because it's pretty.

"Can you believe this jerk?" I extended the butterfly toward Fred. "His ex-girlfriend was killed less than twenty-four hours ago, and he's still harassing me."

Fred pulled rubber gloves from his pocket, leaned down and picked up a tattered envelope. Yes, Henry had worked the envelope over, but gloves seemed a little fastidious even for Fred. "Are you trying not to disturb fingerprints or just being your usual OCD self?"

"Both. Do you mind if I open it?"

That's Fred. Always polite, even at the scene of a stalking. "Sure. Open it, read it, take it home, shred it and burn it. I don't care. I certainly don't want it."

Fred carefully opened the envelope printed with flowers and butterflies then slid out a card with butterflies and hearts on the front. He opened it.

"*Butterflies are free and so are we. Come fly away with me for all eternity. I'll shelter you from harm, and always keep you safe and warm. Anyone who troubles thee will feel the wrath of me.* I didn't know Rick wrote poetry."

"He doesn't. And calling that poetry would be a stretch."

He studied the card carefully. "This doesn't sound like something he would say."

I shrugged. Fred was right. Rick was an idiot, but he was an educated idiot. "Actually, it does sound like something he might write if he was trying to be impossibly cute."

"Or maybe this is from somebody else."

"Who else could it be?"

He turned the card over and looked at the back side which had nothing but the name of a commercial card company. "You tell me."

"It's either Rick or somebody has the wrong house. Maybe they meant to leave this stuff at Sophie's, but their GPS got confused. Mine does that every once in a while. It thinks my friends Judy and Jerry Clarke live in the trash bin at their apartment complex."

Holding the card by the edges, he lifted it to the porch light.

I studied him studying the card. "Can you see fingerprints before you even dust for them?"

"Of course not. I think you need to get some rest."

I could not argue with that. I unlocked my front door, pushed it open, and Henry ran inside. "Good night."

"Good night." Fred scooped up the wrapping paper and ribbon Henry had shredded.

OCD. He wouldn't be able to sleep if he knew there was a mess on my porch.

I watched as he went down the walk. Of course he couldn't just cross the lawns. He might bruise a blade of grass. Or step on an elf. It spoke volumes about his concern for me that he'd walked across the grass beside me.

Then he reached his walk, the decision point. Would he go inside his house or cross the street to Sophie's?

He turned toward me and waved.

I waved back.

He went on up to his house.

Darn! I should have gone inside and watched from the window. If he hadn't seen me, would he have gone to Sophie's? Would he go over after I went in? Would she come to his house? Was it any of my business? Absolutely not. Did I want to know anyway? Oh, yes!

I watched Fred's house until a light came on upstairs. His office, not his bedroom. He was going to get on his computer. Probably planned to illegally hack into government databases and get some more information on Kenneth *Bring us a couple of beers* Wilson.

Or maybe he was going to run down the manufacturer of that card, find the names of everybody who bought one.

I moved to the edge of my porch as if that would give me the ability to see through Fred's blinds.

Surely he was checking on Wilson. Surely this late night activity had nothing to do with his interest in the card and envelope he'd taken with him.

I wished I could unhear his comment about my stalker being somebody other than Rick.

I opened my palm and looked at the butterfly. It sparkled in the moonlight. Of course Rick had brought it. He did that sort of thing when we were dating and after we split up. It was his MO. There was no doubt in my mind that he was responsible for the flowers, wine and crystal butterfly. Though he'd never before written doggerel, I could see him doing that, trying to show me he was an innocent child at heart.

If Fred wanted to amuse himself by fingerprinting the note, that was fine with me. He'd find nothing on there but Rick's fingerprints and Henry's claw marks.

I hoped.

The possibility of a stranger coming onto my porch, leaving gifts and poetry for me…that was too creepy to think about.

A cold wind brushed across my face and sent a chill down my spine. Fall must be closer than I thought.

I hurried into my comfortable, welcoming house which suddenly didn't feel comfortable and welcoming. The moon slanted through the windows creating eerie forms in the darkness. The recliner appeared to have a head sitting atop the headrest. A faded red design on my sofa glowed as if wet with blood. Emptiness flowed down the stairs and across the floor from the kitchen, surrounding me. Henry had vanished somewhere into that emptiness and I was alone.

For a fleeting moment, even though I was still angry at Trent for treating me like a suspect, I wished he was there with me—strong, solid, dependable.

But he wasn't, and I was being silly, letting my imagination run away with me. I switched on the light. I must be experiencing a chocolate deficit to have such ridiculous thoughts. I'd make myself a cup of hot cocoa and go straight to bed.

I went to the kitchen and let out a shriek—just a tiny one—at the sight of eyes glowing in one corner.

Oh, good grief. It was Henry. I flipped on the light, pushing back the darkness and illuminating my cat who stood beside his empty food bowl, looking up with hungry blue eyes. The bowl was designed for a German Shepherd. Henry's a big boy. His head is too large to allow him to eat from a cat dish. Besides, I'd have to refill it at least three times.

"Didn't catch any snacks tonight?" I poured cat food pellets into his bowl, and he purred gratefully.

With my cat happy, I set a cup of milk in the microwave and thought about Tina. She was not likely preparing a cup of hot cocoa in a quiet house. Ken had been pretty drunk when we left, and Fred had brought up Bob's name, reminded him of his wife's infidelity. Did that renew his anger? Did he take out his rage on Tina after Fred and I left? While I stood in my kitchen waiting for my milk to heat, was she waiting to be seen in an emergency room across town?

Or worse?

Would I get a phone call tomorrow asking why I'd visited the recently deceased?

I took the butterfly with me to work the next morning. If I left it at home, Henry would feel the need to track it down and destroy it as he'd done with the flowers. Crystal might be a little harder on his paws and teeth than roses. I sanitized it to get rid of Rickhead's touch and set it in the middle of the top shelf of the dessert display case.

The morning passed uneventfully. Nobody died. Nobody came in and made a scene. People ate their food, left with a smile, and all was well in Death by Chocolate.

Then Brandon's father came in for lunch.

I'm sure I interact with a lot of people who wouldn't be my friends if I knew them on a personal basis. But I don't know them. I ask them what they want to eat and drink, they tell me, I serve it to them, they pay and leave. And life is good.

I could have served Grady Mathis, washed his dishes twice and never given him a second thought if only we could have confined the conversation to, *What would you like today? How about a ham sandwich on moldy bread with rancid mayonnaise*

113

and a glass of anti-freeze? Thank you, here's your order. That didn't happen.

He bellied up to the bar and took a seat on the stool closest to the cash register, the one where I'd have to pass him every time I rang up somebody's check. "Well hello, little lady."

I forced a smile and bit back the urge to tell him I was not little and he should not count on my being a lady. "What can I get for you today, Mr. Mathis?"

He gave a mock frown. I think he intended to look boyish and charming, but he succeeded in looking like a Halloween mask of an ogre. "What's this *Mr. Mathis*? You make me feel old." He reached a hand across the counter, palm up, as if he expected me to put my hand in his. Ewww! "I'm Grady, and you're Lindsay."

I put both hands behind my back and reminded myself, *The customer is always right.* "What can I get for you, *Grady*?"

He ordered a sandwich and drink. "And what wonderful chocolate dessert did you make for me today?"

The customer is always right. "We have the usual chocolate chip cookies and brownies. Our special dessert today is chocolate chip pecan pie."

He grinned and winked. "I'll have the special dessert made by the special lady."

Oh, barf.

"Coming right up." I went back to the kitchen. Unfortunately we had no moldy bread, rancid mayonnaise or antifreeze.

Paula came in while I was making his sandwich. "Do you want me to work the counter awhile?"

"I wouldn't do that to you. I can handle this jerk though I may have to throw a pie in his face rather than serve him a piece."

Paula shook her head. "Don't waste the pie."

She was right. Besides, an iron skillet in his face would be more effective.

I took *Grady's* food to him.

"I see you got a new pretty." He indicated the display case.

What creepy thing was he implying about my desserts?

I turned to look at the case and saw the light winking off the crystal butterfly.

"Oh, that."

"Present from the cop boyfriend?" He winked.

Definitely an iron skillet. A large one. Full of hot grease.

I moved down to the woman two stools away. She'd just finished her brownie. "Would you like anything else?" I asked.

"I sure would." Mathis' words were low, dark and sludgy, like the oil that drains from my car when I haven't changed it for several thousand miles.

I gave the woman her check and she handed me a credit card.

I had to go past the Mathis Monster to get to the credit card machine.

"Boyfriend didn't give you that butterfly, did he?"

I kept my eyes focused on sliding the credit card through the machine and pretended not to hear, but I could feel the flush of anger rising to my cheeks. I really, really wanted to slap him. *The customer is always right.*

I had to pass him on the way back to the customer.

"Cheating on the cop, huh? You are a feisty one!"

The customer is *not* always right. I was going to ask that one to leave, and if he gave me any flack, I knew where the iron skillet was stored. In the interest of haste, I could make do without the hot grease.

I gave the card back to the customer, got her signature, and turned to confront Mathis.

He smiled. "So when are you going to bring that little car in and let me make it all pretty and sexy for you?" He winked again, turning an already slimy question into scum from the depths of a pond that's been stagnant for at least ten years.

When was I going to take my car to his place? Oh, somewhere around the time traffic cops stopped writing tickets. Maybe on the day I started drinking coffee instead of Coke. Sometime after hell froze over in August. I opened my mouth to speak the words.

"Hello, Dad."

I had been so focused on tossing out the father, I hadn't seen the son come in. Wearing a cap with the brim pulled low over his face, he slid onto the stool next to Grady. "Hi, Lindsay."

116

I swallowed my smart-mouth replies. "Hello, Brandon. Good to see you again."

Only one other seat at the counter was occupied, but Brandon chose to sit next to his father. Since they were not best buds, that felt a little confrontational. If Grady Mathis started bullying his son in my restaurant, I would definitely have to get out the iron skillet.

Grady slid off his stool. "Guess I'd better get back to the shop since there's nobody else to take care of it." His voice no longer dripped with slime, but the smug superiority was equally disgusting.

Brandon said nothing, just kept his head bowed, the brim of the cap covering his face.

Grady laid some cash on the counter, looked at me and winked another time. I clenched my fist to keep from punching him in that eye to stop his winking for at least a while. "See you later, little lady."

Not if I see you first. The childish retort almost made it past my lips.

I shuddered and turned my attention to Brandon.

He sat with one elbow on the counter, his hand covering the left side of his face. "I'm sorry about my dad. He can be pushy."

"No problem. I can deal with pushy." It was the obnoxious part I couldn't stand. "What's with the cap?" I grabbed the brim and lifted it…and exposed Brandon's black eye.

He tried to cover it with his hand, but I gently pulled his fingers away. "What happened to you?" I had a horrible feeling I knew what happened to him. I remembered the way his father had talked to him in the shop. Paula had told me her ex-husband began with verbal abuse then moved on to physical.

He shrugged and tried to smile. "Hit my head on a car door."

He was lying. I lie often enough to recognize when somebody else does it. "No, you didn't."

His face brightened to a shade similar to the one I wanted for my car. "I...I..."

"Did your dad do that to you?"

He dropped his gaze.

I slowly lowered my fists to the counter, resisting the urge to slam them down.

"Ma'am," someone called from across the room. "Can I get my check?"

"I'll be right back," I said quietly. "Do not leave."

He looked at me, his brown eyes lighting with happiness and gratitude, reminding me of dogs in animal shelters when someone pats their heads.

Yes, Grady Mathis was destined for an iron skillet encounter.

I gave the customer his check, Paula returned from the kitchen, and I went back to Brandon.

"Tell me what you'd like to eat, and when you're finished, we're going to have a talk."

"Okay," he said quietly, meekly.

I got his order for him, then Paula and I rushed around, taking care of the last of the lunch crowd. While we were both in the kitchen loading dirty dishes in the dishwasher, I had a chance to tell her what was going on.

118

She paused with a plate in her hand, compressed her lips and shook her head. "I don't like Grady Mathis either, but it's not a good idea to interfere in a family fight."

"Wouldn't you have wanted someone to help you when David was abusing you?"

She stood silently for a moment, holding the dirty plate, looking into the distance. Finally she shook her head. "I don't know. I did wish I had a friend to talk to, somebody to help me understand what was happening. But I think I would have resented anyone telling me what I should do."

I took the plate from her and settled it in the dishwasher. "What am I supposed to do? Let that jerk continue to hurt Brandon?"

"Brandon works and lives with his father. When you live with an abuser, it's not always easy to escape. Add the work element, and he's in a bad situation. You can't offer him a place to live and a job. You can't offer him protection."

"I understand," I said, though of course I didn't since I'd never been in that situation. "But I have to try."

Paula laughed softly. "Of course you do. And sometimes that's a good thing. Go talk to him. I'll take care of the two people in the corner and block the door if Brandon tries to run away while you're telling him what to do with his life."

I smiled at the image of Paula tackling Brandon. He was twice as big as she was but I had no doubt she could do it. She'd told me she had once been submissive and helpless but had been forced to learn to be strong to protect her son. She'd learned well.

If Paula could do it, so could Brandon. And maybe I'd check on Tina after work. Invite her to have a drink, talk to her about escaping her abuser. Yes, I'm pushy and bossy and get involved in things that are none of my business. So?

I went out front, moved Brandon's dirty dishes aside and set a piece of chocolate chip pecan pie in front of him. "Eat. You're going to need your strength."

He did as I ordered. Good first step.

I leaned across the counter and spoke quietly. The couple in the corner didn't need to hear our conversation. "Brandon, what your father's doing to you isn't right."

Brandon stared at his plate. "He's my father." The words were wooden and devoid of emotion.

"I don't care. That doesn't give him the right to abuse you. You need to get out of that house, find your own place."

He looked up, his expression hopeful. Maybe all he needed was someone to tell him it was all right to resent that sort of treatment. "But I work for him."

"You can get another job. There are plenty of paint and body shops around, and with your skills, you should have no problem finding employment." I had no idea what his skills were, but since there was a wide range of skill levels in paint and body shops, he was bound to fit in somewhere.

He didn't answer, just sat silently staring at the display case. I suspected he wasn't really seeing anything except inside his head, an image of his terrible plight.

"Don't you want your own home?" I pushed. "Find someone to love you, start a family?"

"Do you have someone to love you?" The question whispered so softly through the air that I barely heard it.

"Well, yes, I think I do." Trent did the *I'm-an-officer-of-the-law* thing to extremes, nagged me about my driving, and generally got on my nerves. But I knew he loved me. And I—

"That's a pretty butterfly." I was wrong. Brandon had been looking at something outside his head, probably to avoid what was going on inside.

I couldn't let him do that. He had to face the situation. "Thank you," I said. "Okay, first we need to find you an apartment."

"Where did you get it?"

"What?"

"The butterfly."

"It was a gift."

"A gift from who? The man who loves you?"

He was trying to change the subject, avoid talking about the actual process of leaving home. I wasn't going to let him do that, and I didn't want to discuss that damned butterfly. I certainly did not want to tell him my sleaze ball ex-husband left it on my porch in the middle of the night. I smiled and shrugged, dismissing the blasted butterfly. "You probably need to find a place across town. Make it as difficult for your father to find you as possible."

"You don't like him, do you?"

"Who?" Were we still talking about that stupid butterfly?

"My dad. Do you like him?"

That was a sticky question. Even though the man was awful, he was Brandon's father. If I said I found him totally disgusting, would Brandon feel the need to defend him and refuse to leave him? I had to think about that one for a moment. "I don't like what your father does to you."

"He likes you."

Three short words that could be taken any number of ways. Considering the flirtatious way Grady Mathis acted, I wondered if Brandon was using *likes* as a synonym for *lusts*?

The phone shrieked. Brandon and I both jumped. I ignored it, knowing Paula would grab it in the kitchen.

"Your father doesn't have the best of manners, but I only have to see him during lunch in a business setting." I gave myself a mental pat on the back for being excruciatingly tactful. It's not something that comes easily for me. "I don't live with him like you do."

Paula emerged from the kitchen. "Lindsay, Trent's on the phone."

"Excuse me," I said to Brandon. "I probably ought to take this." I hated to interrupt our conversation, but Trent only called at work if it was important.

I picked up the phone behind the counter. "Hello?"

"Do you have a minute? Is the rush over?"

"Yes and yes." He didn't sound frantic, but he rarely does.

"Rick's in Pleasant Grove General Hospital. Somebody tried to kill him last night."

Chapter Ten

"Lindsay? Are you there?" Trent's voice sounded miles away. He was miles away.

I swallowed and found my voice. "I'm here."

"Are you all right?"

I stood straighter. "Of course I'm all right. Are you sure somebody tried to murder him? Maybe he's just being dramatic. He's big on being the center of attention."

"It's hard to be dramatic when you're unconscious with a head wound, a broken arm and other contusions."

"I guess it would be tough even for Rickhead to fake something like that," I conceded. "Tough, but not impossible."

"Lindsay, he came close to dying."

"Close only counts when you're dropping an atomic bomb. How'd he get to the hospital? If you tell me he drove himself, I'm going to call *fake*."

"His girlfriend found him in his garage lying next to his car. She was able to keep him alive until the ambulance got there. She's a doctor."

"This is getting to be a habit." I sighed. "Remember a couple of years ago when Bryan Kollar tried to kill him by blowing up his car? Rick really needs to stop being such a jerk that people want to murder him. Is his new girlfriend married?"

"No, but she…" He stopped in mid-sentence.

"But she *what*? Did you just almost tell me something about the *ongoing investigation*? She's dating a member of the mob, right? She's a widow of a member of the mob and she killed her husband. She has an overly protective brother who's a wrestler and takes steroids."

He cleared his throat. "Go meet her yourself. Rick's been asking for you."

"Seriously? He wants me to visit him in the hospital? You'd think he'd be worried I'd finish the job." In the interest of providing possibly useful information, maybe I should tell Trent about Rick's middle-of-the-night gifts. But Brandon was still at the counter, and I didn't want the world to know how completely nuts my ex was. Marrying somebody that crazy reflected badly on my judgment.

"Probably not a good idea to admit to a cop that you might murder your ex-husband," Trent said.

I was pretty sure he was teasing, but it brought up the question of who I was talking to…the cop or my boyfriend. "Got it. So you met the new girlfriend? What kind of doctor is she? Witch doctor? Voodoo doctor? Online degree from the University of Sex on the Beach?"

"Actually, she's a medical doctor, a surgeon."

"You have got to be kidding me. How on earth did somebody with brains enough to be a surgeon get hooked up with Rick?"

"You married him."

"I don't want to talk about that. I have to go now."

"Are you going to the hospital to see him?"

"Well, it probably would be the charitable thing to do."

"Not to mention that you're dying to meet this new girlfriend."

"That too." Actually, that was the only reason I was thinking about going and Trent knew it. There's something both comforting and scary when someone knows you that well.

"Call me tonight and let me know how that goes."

"Okay." I wasn't about to share information with him if he wouldn't share information with me.

He laughed and hung up. Good grief. Had he also figured out what *okay* meant?

"Everything all right?" Brandon asked. He hadn't finished his pie. Apparently he'd been listening very intently to my conversation.

I refilled his glass of tea. "Pretty much. Somebody tried unsuccessfully to kill my ex-husband."

"I gathered that from what you said. Sorry, I didn't mean to eavesdrop."

I smiled. "It'd be hard not to when I'm only a couple of feet away."

"Is he going to live?"

"I guess so. His girlfriend found him in time and saved his life. But he could still get a staph infection or the jealous husband could try again and succeed."

Brandon laughed. That was good. I suspected he didn't laugh nearly enough.

"Okay," he said, "getting back to more important things, where do we start looking for this new apartment?"

Wow! That was easy. I usually have to argue with people a long time to convince them to do things my way. "How about Kansas City North? That should be far enough away from your father."

A wide grin spread across his face. His black eye was a little incongruous with the happy expression, but it was better than if he'd been frowning with a black eye. "One bedroom or two?"

"Umm, well, you could start with one bedroom then move up to two when you need more space."

I wouldn't have thought it possible, but his smile became even wider. "When I have a wife and family. Then I'll need a house."

He was really running with this thing. Maybe a little too fast. Maybe his expectations were unrealistic. "One step at a time. First the apartment, then a new job, then a house."

He nodded. "You have a house."

"I do, yes. A small house. I got it in the divorce. Before I married Rick, I lived in an apartment."

"I see." He laid some bills on the counter and slid off his stool. "I'm going to go find an apartment right now."

"Great! Uh, don't you have to go back to work?"

"I'm not going to let my dad push me around anymore."

"I see. Okay. Good." At least, I hoped that was good. I was afraid the break was going to be more difficult than Brandon realized.

He strode out the door then turned to smile and wave.

"That intervention was certainly successful," Paula said.

I hadn't noticed her come in from the kitchen, but she's sneaky like that. "You were eavesdropping."

"A skill I learned from you."

"You think he's really going to do it?" I asked.

"I don't know. It seemed too easy. His excitement may wear off when he sees how tough it's going to be."

"That's what I'm worried about. He seemed so pumped and eager."

She shook her head. "He's not going to do it. Not yet anyway."

"Probably not," I agreed. "But I've planted the seed."

"You've got to be patient and supportive with him. Most people who leave abusive situations make several false starts before they finally escape." Her voice was soft, but the force of it filled the room.

"Of course I'll be supportive. I can't believe you'd even question that."

"Sometimes you get a little impatient."

"I don't remember ever doing that." We both knew it was a lie. There's nothing wrong with my memory. "Let's get this place cleaned up. I'm going to the hospital to visit Rickhead and accidentally trip and fall on his wounded body parts."

"You're going to see his new girlfriend."

"Did you hear? She's a doctor! A real doctor, not a witch doctor. What on earth can she possibly see in him?"

Paula smirked. "You married him."

"That's the second time today some rude person has pointed that out to me." I grabbed Brandon's dirty dishes and headed for the kitchen.

❧

Bandages and bruises covered most of Rick's head, chest and arms. The unbandaged parts had tubes attached making him look like a mechanical octopus.

He smiled wanly with the side of his face that wasn't bandaged. "Lindsay, you came." His voice was quiet and a little slurred. Pain, medication or swelling? Probably all of the above.

I moved closer to the bed. "You don't look so good. How do you feel?"

"Good. I feel good now that you're here."

"What happened? Trent said somebody tried to kill you. Who'd you piss off this time?"

He made a strange sound that was probably meant to be a laugh. Hard to laugh when half your face is bandaged. "That's my Lindsay. Call it like you see it. You never let me down."

I wasn't sure if that was a compliment or an insult. "So what happened? Somebody shove you under a bus?"

"The scumbag hid in my garage. In my own garage! Jumped me when I got out of the car. But I fought him. Got in a few punches before I went down." He lifted his left hand, the bruised,

129

unbandaged one with an IV dangling from it. "Police are checking all the hospitals. He won't get far in the condition I left him in."

I refrained from pointing out that physicality was not one of Rick's strong points. His nine year old son bragged that he beat his dad at arm wrestling. Rick said he let the boy win. Rick never *let* anybody win.

"I'm sure they'll catch him soon. Did you get a good look at him?"

"No. Coward hit me from behind. In my own garage!"

He was hung up on the garage thing. "Could be worse. It could have been in your own bathroom."

The half smile lit his face again. Was he really laughing at my humor?

No. A female doctor had entered his room, a drop dead gorgeous female doctor. Tall and willowy with dark skin and short black curls, she could have been on the cover of a fashion magazine instead of wearing a white coat and stethoscope.

"Hi, Robin," Rick said.

"Hello, Rick. How are you doing?" She gave him a wide smile and moved to the other side of his bed to check one of the monitors.

"Robin, Lindsay. Lindsay, Robin. Ex-wife, meet next wife."

Robin? This gorgeous woman was the doctor/girlfriend Trent mentioned? I studied her carefully to see if I could spot the defect that made her think Rick was an appropriate partner.

The model masquerading as a doctor turned her dazzling smile on me. "Hello, Lindsay. I thought that might be you. Rick's told me so much about you."

"Oh, well, uh…"

"Isn't she beautiful, Lindsay?" Rick asked. "Will you marry me, Robin?"

Doctor Robin made an adjustment to one of Rick's IVs. "He's a little loopy right now. We've got him on a lot of pain medication."

"I didn't notice any difference from his sober state. How's he doing?"

"He came through the surgery quite well. It's going to be a while before he's completely healed, but he's on his way."

"I got a great doctor. She saved my life."

"I heard," I said.

"If she hadn't come in and found me when I didn't answer the door, I'd be dead."

She smoothed the sheet over him and squeezed his fingers gently then looked at me. "I knew something wasn't right as soon as I pulled into the driveway. It was starting to get dark, but there were no lights in his house. He didn't answer the doorbell or his cell phone. I found a key in that fake rock beside the front porch and went inside." She looked down at him fondly. "That's not a very good place to hide a key."

That fake rock had been my contribution, but Rick was too drugged to point that out. I certainly wasn't going to.

"So you found him in the garage?" Yes, that was an established fact, but it was better than blurting out, *You're dating him? You can do so much better!*

Her dark eyes clouded. "He was unconscious and in bad shape. Someone had beaten him with a pipe wrench. I didn't think he was going to make it."

"I hit him back," Rick said.

"I know you did. You were very brave." She laid a hand on his shoulder and gazed at him lovingly.

Gag.

Very strange situation. I liked Rick's new girlfriend, but I doubted we'd ever become bosom buddies because I didn't like Rick.

"Well. I'm glad he's safe and in good hands. I'd better get home and feed my cat. I hope they find whoever did this."

"If Rick hurt the attacker as badly as he believes he did, the police should be able to find his DNA. There was a lot of blood."

"I hurt him. Made him cry like a baby. I think it was Martian Man."

Martian Man? "He really is on a lot of drugs. Is this a flashback to a sci-fi movie?"

Robin grimaced. "That's what he calls my former boyfriend, Martin. We spotted Martin in a restaurant the other night, and Rick was convinced he was following me."

Not a jealous husband, but it could be a jealous ex-lover. Was that what Trent had almost slipped up and told me? "Was your breakup a bad one?"

She nodded. "Very bad."

"Was he violent?"

She looked toward the door as though checking to see if anyone else was listening. "He's a doctor too," she said quietly. "He was a wonderful person until he started prescribing medication for himself. That's why we broke up. He was becoming more and more aggressive. I got out before he reached the violent stage, but, yes, it's possible. The police are looking at him as a person of interest."

"I've been one of those," I said. "It's not as much fun as you might think."

She laughed.

Yeah, under other circumstances, we might be friends.

"Take care of him. I'll check back tomorrow."

"Thanks for coming by, Lindsay. It was nice to finally meet you."

"Love you, Lindsay!" Rick called. "Love you more, Robin. Will you marry me?"

He really did seem totally besotted with her. Too besotted to be leaving gifts on my front porch?

I started out the door then stopped as something niggled at my brain, something that didn't quite fit in place. "You said it was getting dark when you found Rick."

Dr. Robin lifted her gaze from the notes she was making on a clipboard. "Yes. I got to his house around seven."

"Seven o'clock. Twilight but not dark."

"Does that mean something?" Robin asked.

"No, no. Just curious. Have a good evening."

Something was off. I could believe Rick would be crazy enough to leave a gift on my porch even though he was in love with somebody else. But in order to get back to his place, be attacked, fight off the attacker, and lie bleeding until Robin found him, he'd have had to do it in broad daylight and risk being seen by someone. Rick always made his gift-giving trips in the middle of the night.

I stopped dead in the middle of the hospital corridor, almost causing a collision with a nurse. She frowned at me and hurried on her way. Other nurses and visitors flowed around me, anonymous faces, people I'd never seen before and didn't really see then.

Rick had not inquired if I enjoyed his gifts, something he always did after leaving them.

I had to consider the possibility that Rick was lying in his garage bleeding or in the hospital on drugs when that butterfly appeared on my porch.

For once Rick might be innocent. Somebody else could have left the butterfly, the flowers and the wine. A stranger could be watching me, writing stupid poems for me, coming onto my porch, to the back door of my restaurant, invading my space, leaving unwelcome gifts.

Chapter Eleven

I walked out of the hospital to find that the sky had clouded over and the air held a damp chill. Winter was on its way. That seemed appropriate.

I drove home in a hyper-alert daze. Yes, I know that sounds contradictory, but it's the only way I can explain it. Every time a car was behind me for more than a block, I looked in the rearview mirror and tried to memorize the license plate, then turned down a side street to see if the car would follow. Once I thought somebody in a car in front of me looked vaguely familiar, but decided that was a little paranoid. It's difficult to follow somebody from in front.

It took me a long time to get home.

When I reached my neighborhood, I peered through the gathering shadows of evening at people walking their dogs, at every tree in case somebody was hiding behind it, inside every car parked in a driveway or on the street. Since I live in a neighborhood built before the days of attached garages, there were a lot of cars parked on the street.

I turned into my driveway and got out. Early darkness hovered around the edges of the clouds overhead and around my house and yard. My oak tree loomed ominously, its trunk big enough to hide somebody. I really should have trimmed those bushes

135

at the back of my house. A whole gang of stalkers could be hiding in them.

I shivered. Not because I was scared, of course, but because the air was a little chilly.

Okay, it's possible some of that chill was inside me rather than outside. Hard to tell.

I put my car in the garage, closed the door and wished I could lock it. Not that it mattered. A solid push would bring down the entire structure.

So far my out-of-season Santa Claus had left gifts on my front porch at home and my back door at work. But who knew what he was going to do next? Climb a ladder to my bedroom window? Be waiting in the back seat of my car when I left for work? He'd have to be extremely short to do that, but short people can be dangerous too.

Light glowed from Paula's living room and kitchen windows. Fred's house was dark, which didn't mean he wasn't there. He has blackout shades and heavy curtains on all his windows. Across the street Sophie's house was also dark. As far as I knew, she didn't have blackout shades. They wouldn't have fit with the décor.

I headed toward the darkness of my front door. As soon as I fed Henry, I could go to Paula's, hang out, visit with Zach. Or I could go over and knock on Fred's door, see if his blackout shades were drawn and he was working or if he and Sophie were over there in the darkness doing what people do in the darkness.

Not that I was trying to avoid my own home. I just felt certain Paula would want to know about

Rick's condition, and I needed to talk to Fred, tell him about my epiphany that Rick hadn't been leaving the gifts. Judging from the meticulous way he'd collected the wrapping paper and note card, he probably already suspected that. If he found fingerprints, he might know it for certain. Maybe he'd researched the fingerprint database and already knew who my stalker was. A visit to Fred was definitely in order.

Okay, to be honest, I felt creepy about going into my house. Having Rickhead around the last couple of years, spying on me, popping up at odd moments such as in my shower when he was supposed to be dead had been freaky enough. Knowing somebody was watching me and coming onto my porch while I slept in the room above with my window open was every bit as unnerving as the time people kept breaking into my basement.

I straightened my spine and resolved not to let some sicko make me scared of my own home. I opened the front door and Henry dashed out, gave me one head butt, then turned and stalked toward the kitchen. I was late and he was hungry. My fears abated. Henry's calm demeanor told me no intruder was in the house or on the porch.

I dropped my purse on the coffee table and went straight to the kitchen.

He sat beside his empty bowl, looking at me accusingly.

I retrieved his dry food from the pantry and filled his bowl then added a dollop of smelly canned food as a treat since he'd had to wait so long.

Sally Berneathy

As soon as I set it on the floor, he dove in.

I got out a chunk of cheese and some crackers then sat down at the table and made dinner conversation. "Remember Rickhead, the guy you don't like? Well, he almost got killed."

Henry continued to eat noisily, but I knew from his occasional snort that he was listening. I told him all about Rick and his new girlfriend.

"No idea what she sees in him. Maybe her friends dared her to find the lowest piece of pond scum around and date him."

"Anlinny!"

I screamed and whirled at the sound of a voice behind me. For an instant my heart tried to climb into my throat, but in the next instant it went back down where it belonged. Only one person calls me Anlinny, kid-speak for Aunt Lindsay. Paula's three year old son, Zach.

The boy hurled himself at me and grabbed me around the leg. "You got cookies?"

With a hand that shook only slightly, I tousled his soft blond hair. "For you, I can probably find a few. They may be old and moldy."

"Okay." He released me and petted Henry who continued to eat.

Paula came into the room. "I'm sorry. Zach was so eager to see you, he ran ahead. Apparently your door was unlocked so he invited himself in."

"I left my front door unlocked? Oh, great!" I started for the living room, but Paula stopped me.

"I locked it. I tried to turn on your porch light too, but it's burned out."

138

"I'll replace the bulb." I definitely wanted to do that. I'd leave it on all night and hope the light would be a deterrent to anyone sneaking onto my property.

Paula held up a bottle of white wine. "I thought you might be upset so I brought some comfort."

"Bless you! You grab the glasses, and I'll get some cookies and juice for Zach."

I found a chocolate chip cookie and handed it to Zach along with a glass of white grape juice.

"Is my cookie moldy?" he asked.

"Of course." It wasn't.

He smiled and accepted the cookie and juice. "My wine?"

"Yep. Try not to get too drunk. You're the designated driver."

He nodded solemnly. "Okay."

Paula stood at the counter, uncorking the real bottle of wine. "Sit at the table so you don't spill your drink on the floor."

I wasn't sure if she was talking to me or Zach, but he obediently took a seat at my kitchen table.

Paula poured the wine and we took seats at the table on each side of Zach. I lifted my glass and drank half of it in one gulp.

"That bad, huh?" Paula asked.

I nodded.

Paula sipped her wine. "I was afraid it would be. You're not as tough as you pretend to be."

I frowned. "Am too." I lifted my glass for another gulp.

Paula laughed softly. "I just meant that it's normal to be upset when you realize somebody you once loved almost died."

I choked on my wine, spit some on the table and went into a laughing, coughing fit.

Paula grabbed a napkin and cleaned the table. "Are you okay?"

I cleared my throat and wiped tears from my eyes. "You think I'm freaked out because Rickhead almost got killed? Were you upset when they hauled David off to prison?"

"That's different. He tried to take Zach, have me sent to prison, and kill you. I hated him for a long time before I escaped from him. But when you and Rick first split up, you were... um...*distraught* about the separation."

I took another sip of wine. "That's the thing about long-time friends. You remember things I'd rather forget. Well, it's been quite a while since I've been *distraught*."

"So Rick's not the reason you just drank half a glass of wine without tasting it?"

"In a way, but not the way you're thinking." I told her about Rick's new girlfriend and the fact that it was unlikely he'd left the crystal butterfly on my porch. "If we assume the same person left all the gifts and stupid poems, it would seem I have a secret admirer, aka a stalker."

Paula shuddered. "And you left your front door unlocked tonight."

"Henry met me, hungry but not excited the way he gets when somebody comes around who shouldn't be here. Besides, I don't obsess about locking my door. This is usually such a safe neighborhood."

"Sure, except for the time my ex-husband tried to kill you in your own living room, and the time Tiger Lily almost murdered you in your bedroom. And how about Jay Jamison breaking into Sophie's house and almost killing you?"

"Yeah, yeah, yeah. I plan to be very careful about locking all my doors from now on."

"Why don't you and Henry come over and spend the night with us?"

"Oboy! Can Henry come to my house?" Zach asked.

"Sometime," I replied.

"Can I have another moldy cookie?"

"Sometime," Paula said. She set her glass on the table and rose. "Young man, you need to go to bed."

Zach's blue eyes twinkled as he looked up at his mother. "Sometime."

Paula grinned. "*Sometime* comes in fifteen minutes. Up!" She turned to me. "Coming with us?"

"Thanks, but I don't think so. As long as Henry's here, I'll be fine."

"At least call Trent and Fred and tell them."

"I think Fred already knows. Last night he took the note and wrapping paper home with him. It's possible he was just being tidy, but I think he knew the gifts weren't coming from Rick."

She nodded. "If Fred knows, I won't worry about you. He'll keep watch. Probably has a camera trained on your front porch right now."

I made a mental note not to go outside naked.

Henry accompanied us to the door and strolled out into the night, searching for fun and adventure as well as gifts for me. "Hurry back," I called after his ghostly form. He swished his tail. I interpreted that as agreement.

Paula looked up at my dark porch light. "Don't forget to change the bulb. Now, while I'm still here."

"You're awfully bossy." I reached up to unscrew the old bulb. It was loose. I screwed it in, turned on the switch, and the light came on.

I looked at Paula.

She looked at me. "Someone loosened your light bulb so it wouldn't work. So he could hide in the dark."

I swallowed hard. "We don't know that. Maybe it came loose on its own. Maybe it's been slowly coming loose for some time and finally reached the critical point today."

"Are you sure you don't want to come home with us?"

"Henry wants to come home with me." Zach's voice was sleepy and he leaned against his mother's leg.

I ruffled his hair. "Had too much wine, didn't you, Hot Shot?"

"Uh huh," he mumbled.

"I'll be fine. Thank you for coming over." I hugged Paula. "That's another thing about long-time friends. You know when I need you."

"Hug, Anlinny." Zach's eyelids drooped as he lifted his arms to me.

I reached down and picked him up. "You better ease up on the moldy cookies or soon I won't be able to lift you."

He giggled, wrapped his arms around my neck and gave me a kiss on the cheek. "I love you, Anlinny."

I kissed his forehead. "Love you back."

I watched until Paula and Zach were inside their house with the door closed. Paula had three locks on her front door. Perhaps I should follow her example.

With the porch light on, I felt as if I were standing in the spotlight, easily visible to whoever was out there. I turned it off.

The cloudy, moonless night wrapped its darkness around me. Maybe I should have gone home with Paula. I suddenly felt very alone and vulnerable.

"Henry!"

I saw no sign of my cat. The only movement was a dark sedan turning onto my street a few blocks away, its headlights spearing through the darkness toward me.

"Henry! Come here! Now!" I tried to control my voice, tried not to freak out just because a car was driving down my street. My neighbors could be coming home after going to a movie. Or they could have visitors. I wasn't the only person who lived on that street.

The sedan came closer.

I held my breath, waiting for it to stop in front of somebody else's house.

Like a ghost in the darkness, Henry sauntered over from Fred's yard. The two of them pretended they didn't like each other, but it wouldn't have surprised me to find they were meeting in secret.

"Do you think you could move a little faster?" The sedan was a block away and, against all reason, I was starting to panic.

Apparently Henry did not think he needed to move any faster. I knew he could because I'd seen him streak across the yard when he was hungry. That night he moseyed.

The sedan came to a stop in front of my house.

Was this my stalker? Was he going to leave something on my porch? Could he not see me in the dark? Maybe I should turn on the porch light. But if he saw me, what would he do?

Funny how the night was no longer chilly. I was beginning to perspire.

Henry leapt onto my porch like a graceful, unhurried ballerina.

I held the screen door open. "Inside. Now."

He strolled casually, obviously not feeling my sense of urgency. That was a good thing, probably meant the car held no danger.

Even so, I wanted to get in the house and lock the door.

"Hurry." I almost stepped on Henry's tail in my eagerness to get inside.

A car door slammed. My heart stuttered then went into overdrive.

I reached down to give Henry's fuzzy rear a push so I could get far enough in to close the door.

"Lindsay!"

For an instant I couldn't breathe. For an instant I wondered if Henry had gone senile and would no longer warn me about threats.

But I knew that voice. I spun around. Trent strode up the sidewalk, resplendent in faded blue jeans, sports coat and a big smile.

I stepped back outside. "Hi." I tried to sound calm, as if I hadn't just been planning to barricade myself in the house. "You gave me a start. Where'd you get that ugly car?"

"It's the department's. I was working late tonight and needed to be inconspicuous."

As if his regular car, a newer model black sedan, was conspicuous.

He stepped onto the porch and handed me a gold box. Godiva chocolates. "I thought you might need some chocolate you didn't have to make."

I accepted the box, threw my arms around him and held on tight. I didn't want to seem needy, so I pulled back much sooner than I wanted to.

"Can we continue this inside?" I asked. "The neighbors get so uptight when we have sex on the front porch."

He grinned. "How about the back porch?"

"That'll work."

I led him inside, closed and locked the door behind us. Even with a cop on the premises, I didn't want to take any chances.

"Coke? Wine? Beer? Coffee?"

Trent sank onto the sofa and made a face. "You make the worst coffee I've ever tasted, and I'm driving so alcohol is out. How about a glass of water and a cookie?"

"I have some moldy chocolate chip cookies."

"What?"

"Never mind. Private joke between Zach and me. I have cookies and water."

I set the Godiva box on the coffee table and went to the kitchen where I found Henry begging for catnip. He's addicted, but who am I to talk? I can't imagine going through a day without chocolate and Cokes. "Tonight you need to be alert and protect me." However, thinking about my chocolate and Coke addictions, I gave him a tiny amount. Wouldn't want him to go into withdrawal.

I got a bottle of water for Trent, a Coke for me and a plate of cookies then went back to the living room.

"How are you doing?" Trent asked softly as I handed him the water and a cookie.

I hadn't told him anything about my personal Santa Claus, so he must be talking about Rick. Good grief.

I sat beside him, opened the gold box and selected the Dark Ganache Heart. "I'm fine. Why do you ask?" I slid the candy into my mouth and savored the dark, smooth chocolate. A fresh box of Godiva chocolates and Trent beside me. Life was good.

He lifted an eyebrow. "Why? Well, let's see. Last night your ex-husband was almost killed. Your friend was murdered in the alley behind your restaurant. Your ex-husband's ex-girlfriend was

146

murdered in front of his house and you're a person of interest. Most people would find that upsetting."

"I am upset about Bob and a little bit about Ginger. Have you figured out who killed either of them yet?"

I selected another candy and offered the box to Trent but he smiled and took another cookie. "I like the chocolates my girlfriend makes better than the store bought stuff."

"Aw, that's sweet. Now answer my question. Who killed Bob and Ginger?"

He munched on his cookie.

I popped open my Coke with a loud snap. "Oh, for crying out loud! Do not give me that business about not being able to talk about an ongoing investigation. I just want to know what I'd hear on the ten o'clock news if I watched the ten o'clock news, which I don't. But I can always Google it if you keep holding out on me."

"That's not what I was going to say, but it does apply." He leaned back on the sofa and focused on the label on his bottle of water, avoiding my eyes. "The investigation of Bob's death has reached a dead end."

"Did you talk to Kenneth Wilson?"

He lifted his gaze to mine and frowned. "Yeah, I did. We just uncovered that connection today. How did you know—oh, Fred."

"He looks guilty to me. Kenneth, not Fred."

"Kenneth Wilson has an alibi. His wife swears he was with her all night."

I snorted. "She's so scared of him, she'd say he was with her the day she was born if he told her to."

Trent nodded. "I know. But we have no evidence that points to him. I'm sorry, but unless a new lead turns up, we don't have anything to investigate. The case has gone cold."

"If he'd been a rich executive, you wouldn't stop looking for his killer."

"If we ran out of leads, we would."

I thumped my can of Coke down on the coffee table. "Fred and I aren't going to stop."

Trent's lips tightened. "I really wish you'd back off and let us handle things."

"I would if you were handling things, but you're not. You just said you don't have any leads on Bob's case."

"Because we don't. Do you?"

I hate it when he uses logic against me. "I can't discuss an ongoing investigation."

He laughed. "Okay, let's leave that subject and get back to talking about your ex-husband who was almost murdered, the man you went to visit in the hospital."

"I think we'd better leave that subject too. You told me it was a bad idea to tell a cop I wanted to murder my ex-husband. How about we move on to the weather?"

"So you're not the least bit upset that a man you once loved almost died? It's normal if you are. It doesn't bother me."

"I'm not. I promise."

"Really? I could have sworn, judging from the desperate way you looked at me when I walked up and the way you held on while we were outside, that you were a little stressed."

"Well, maybe, sort of. Except not like you think. I'm upset because Rick didn't leave the gifts for me."

Trent looked confused. "You wanted Rick to leave you gifts?"

"No, of course not. I was angry with him for doing it except it wasn't him. It couldn't have been him. He was lying in his garage bleeding or maybe even in the ambulance on the way to the hospital when someone left the butterfly. *That's* why I'm upset. I could care less if Rick lives or dies."

Trent looked as if he'd just watched an Akira Kurosawa movie without English dubbing.

"Maybe I better start at the beginning," I said.

"That would be a good idea. And I think I'll have a beer after all."

I started to get up, but he put a hand on my arm. "Stay here. I know where the refrigerator is. Don't go anywhere. Stay right here."

"Where would I go? This is my house."

Henry leapt onto the sofa and sat close to me. I petted him and he purred. Listening to the sound of the ocean is relaxing, but it doesn't come close to listening to a cat purring.

Trent returned with a beer and resumed his seat next to me. "All right. Tell me about the gifts Rick didn't give you."

I told him the whole story, from the roses to the butterfly, ending with my realization that it was

149

probable some stranger had been trespassing on my property.

"And the reason you're just now telling me this would be…?"

I shrugged and reached for another piece of candy. Confessions require chocolate. "I thought it was Rickhead."

I watched his eyes and saw the evolution from boyfriend to cop. It wasn't what I wanted to see. "You didn't think the whole situation was a little strange?"

"Strange, sure, but normal for Rick. He's done it before."

"So the first two gifts and notes have been destroyed, but you have the butterfly, the wrapping paper and the note?"

He was all cop. My boyfriend had left the building. I needed comfort and cuddling, but I was going to get an inquisition. "The butterfly's at the restaurant, and Fred's got the wrapping paper and note."

"What's Fred doing with them?"

I spread my hands. "Seriously? You want me to speculate on what Fred's doing with that stuff? Maybe he's checking it for fingerprints and DNA. Maybe he's using the back of it for scratch paper to make notes of what the voices in his head tell him. Maybe he's developed a process to turn paper into gold."

"Lindsay, this is serious. We need that wrapping paper, the note and the butterfly."

"You're probably not going to find much on the butterfly. I cleaned and sanitized it."

He sighed. "And you call Fred OCD?"

"Hey! I put it in the display case with my cookies. I didn't want Rick's DNA anywhere near food."

"I'd still like to look at it. Can you get the paper and note from Fred and bring them to the station tomorrow along with the butterfly?"

"Of course I can. What you should be asking is, will I?"

He smiled, set his beer on the coffee table and took both my hands in his. I was pleased to see flashes of green in the darkness of his eyes. My boyfriend was back. "Will you bring those items to me tomorrow?"

"Sure. After you leave, I'll go to Fred's and ask him." And see if Sophie was there. Now I had a legitimate excuse for snooping.

He pulled me close. "I'm not leaving."

I snuggled into his warmth, into his familiar arms. "I'm good with that. Not that I need a body guard, but I like sleeping with you."

"Of course you don't need a body guard. I would never suggest that."

"Good." I leaned back and cuddled against him.

He wrapped his arm around my shoulders and was quiet long enough for me to relax and let my guard down. "So if Rick didn't leave the gifts, who did?"

He couldn't stop playing cop. "I have no idea. Isn't that your job, to find out?"

151

"I plan to do that. But this may be somebody you know. Has anybody been extra friendly lately? A neighbor? Somebody at the restaurant leave big tips? Ask you personal questions?"

Ask you personal questions?

The words evoked an image of a wide face with pock-marked skin and bushy brows low over narrow eyes that leered and winked.

"Boyfriend didn't give you that butterfly, did he?"

"I'll have the special dessert made by the special lady."

"You are a feisty little thing!"

"There is a disgusting creep that's been in Death by Chocolate a couple of times. I don't know if he's my stalker, but he's awful. His name is Grady Mathis."

"Grady Mathis? Who is he? How do you know him?" The cop again, but this time I didn't mind, was almost glad.

Had Grady Mathis been on my porch, peeking into my window? The thought made me shudder. I'd have to scrub my porch thoroughly. Suddenly some of Fred's OCD actions made sense.

I told Trent about the car repair shop and how Grady had acted in the restaurant, including what he asked me about the butterfly. He had shown an interest in it and had seemed certain my *boyfriend didn't give you that butterfly, did he?*

Trent shook his head. "I wish you'd told me about these incidents when they happened."

I frowned. "Seriously? You think I should have told you that I thought Rickhead was leaving gifts again and that a rude customer flirted with me? Not my idea of pillow talk." I settled back into his arms. "Anyway, this whole thing only started on Monday night *after* you and Lawson were over here, so other than when you hauled me into the station and had Lawson grill me about Ginger, I haven't had a chance to talk to you. Oh, wait. Never mind. If it started on Monday, it can't be Grady. I went to Mathis Paint and Body Shop on Tuesday. That's the first time I met him."

"Stalkers often obsess about someone they've seen but never actually met. Are you sure he hadn't been in Death by Chocolate before you met him on Tuesday?"

When I first saw Brandon's father I had a feeling I'd seen him before but assumed it was because there was a father-son resemblance. "I don't know. He could have been. Their place of business isn't very far from mine. In one day I see hundreds of faces. Brandon knew me, but I didn't remember him."

"Brandon's the son, the one who ran into your car and convinced you to come to their shop in the first place?"

"Yes."

"Maybe Brandon's involved in all this. Maybe the father and son are in this together, and Brandon staged the accident to get you into their shop."

Trent's a cop and he knows about these things, but I couldn't buy into that theory. "No way.

Brandon's a big, soft-spoken teddy bear. He'd never do something like that."

"I'll run a background check on both of them in the morning—"

"Brandon's clean but Grady has two DUIs and he's been in trouble for sexual harassment."

Trent stiffened and gave me the cop stare. "And you know this how?"

Oops. I lifted my chin and gave him the obstinate red head stare. "I'm psychic."

"Fred, of course. So you knew about this guy's background and you still didn't tell me he was bothering you?"

I threw up my hands and sighed dramatically. "I just told you, and you're making me sorry I did!" The best defense is a good offense. "If you harbor any illusions of getting personal with me tonight, you'll give up the cop attitude and go back to being Trent."

He looked thoughtful for a moment then nodded. "Tonight I'll be your boyfriend. Tomorrow morning the cop will have a talk with Mathis."

I started to protest. Mathis hadn't done anything wrong except be obnoxious. However, it would be nice not to ever see him again. "I'd rather my boyfriend had the talk. Just make it clear to him that you and I are involved and you carry a gun and you're very jealous."

He laughed. "I think I can probably get the message across. But if he comes back to the restaurant, call Detective Adam Trent immediately." He rose and took my hand. "Now, about that getting personal stuff..."

I cleared our snacks off the coffee table and put away the cookies then set the box of Godiva chocolates on the top shelf of my pantry, partly to hide it from Henry and partly to hide it from me. If it was visible, I'd eat the entire box before I left for work in the morning.

We started upstairs and Henry dashed ahead. Instead of going straight to the foot of my bed, he curled in the corner. He may be a catnip-aholic, but he has good manners.

☜❤☞

I was sleeping soundly and happily when Trent's freaking cell phone rang.

He groaned and rolled over, uncurling himself from my back, taking away the warm.

I looked at the clock. Six minutes after two a.m. Probably not his dentist's office with a reminder call.

He grabbed his phone off the nightstand. "Adam Trent...Yes...I see...I will...I'm on my way." He laid the phone back on the nightstand and rolled over to wrap his arms around me.

I returned the embrace. "I'm going to take a wild guess and say you're on your way somewhere besides my bed."

He sighed. "I'm sorry."

"Oh, well. Better a few hours of fun than no fun at all." I kissed him then shoved him away. "Get dressed. Go play cop."

"Lindsay, I need to tell you what that call was about." Even in the dark, I could see that he had that *I'm so sorry, ma'am, but I have bad news* look on his face.

My breath caught in my chest. Had somebody else been killed? Somebody I knew?

"Somebody tried again to kill Rick."

I breathed a huge sigh of relief. "Oh, thank goodness!"

He frowned. "What?"

"I mean, thank goodness it wasn't somebody else, somebody I care about." Trent's frown didn't clear, so I hurried on to another question. "What happened?"

"I don't have all the details yet. Someone hit him on the head with something heavy. He's in emergency surgery again, but they think he's going to be okay."

"Really? If I'd known a couple of whacks over the head would make him *okay*, I'd have done that to him years ago."

He got out of bed and started putting on his clothes. "Sometime we need to talk about this attitude you have toward your ex-husband."

"I think it's a perfectly normal attitude. What's your attitude toward your ex-wife? How would you feel if she'd just been almost murdered twice? Wouldn't you kind of wish the killer had been a little more competent?" I got up and pulled on my jeans.

"Go back to bed. I know my way out."

"No, you might get lost. Besides, I need to lock the deadbolt behind you."

"True."

We walked downstairs.

"I think I just made a good point," I said. "The killer isn't very competent, is he?"

"You mean because he failed twice to kill Rick?"

We reached the front door and I turned the deadbolt to unlock it. "That too, but if you think about it, he could have put an air bubble in Rick's IV. He could have posed as a doctor and given him a shot of insulin. Instead, he just whacked him over the head again. Brute force."

"You watch too much television." He gave me a quick goodnight kiss. "Don't come out. Lock up behind me, turn your porch light on and go straight to bed."

For once, I was willing to take orders.

I flipped on the light and stood in the doorway watching him as he strode down the sidewalk.

Clouds still covered the moon and thunder rumbled somewhere in the distance. If it rained, surely my stalker would stay home.

I waved as Trent drove away.

I'd felt safe while he was with me. When he left, I felt very exposed, as if unseen eyes were watching me, as if Mathis or some stranger was going to pop out from behind a tree at any moment.

The thunder rumbled louder. A chilly autumn wind blew my hair across my face and sent shivers down my spine.

I strained to see behind bushes, around the thick trunk of the oak tree, in the shadows of Paula's house next door and Sophie's house across the street. I didn't bother to look at Fred's house. Between his psychic ability and his x-ray vision, not to mention all sorts of electronic microphones and cameras, he'd know if anyone came close to his house.

I couldn't see anybody.

If I was inside with the blinds closed, nobody could see me.

I stepped back, shut the door and turned the deadbolt.

Lightning flashed, briefly illuminating the living room and turning the lamp, sofa, chair and television into evil aliens. Thunder crashed.

I ran upstairs where Henry waited on the foot of my bed. He was calm. If Henry was calm, everything was fine.

I turned off the lamp and went to the window. Tree branches thrashed about in the wind. Lightning streaked through the sky, bringing shadows to life and sending them dancing across my yard.

I considered closing my window. Not to shut out the storm. I love a good thunderstorm. No, I wanted to shut out those shadows. However, at the same time I wanted to hear if somebody came on my porch. I wanted to catch him in the act and dump Henry's litter box on his head.

I left the window up.

My phone rang and I almost jumped out of my skin.

I looked at the display.

Fred?

Lightning flashed. Thunder boomed a split second later. The storm was getting closer.

My heart rate sped up. It was a strange hour for anyone to call, even Fred. Was he calling to warn me about something or someone he'd seen skulking around my house?

I picked up my phone. "Fred?"

"Of course it's me. Who else would be calling from my cell phone?"

I released a long breath. He didn't sound as if he was worried about my safety. He sounded like his usual snarky self. "Why are you calling at this hour?"

"I saw you were up and wanted to be sure you were okay. I can come over if you want me to since Trent had to leave."

I laughed. "Even if I were scared—which I'm not—I don't need you to come over because you're already watching everything that goes on over here."

"I wish that were true. If it was, I'd have seen that creep who left the roses. I do sleep sometimes."

"You do?"

He ignored my question. "I have more bad news. I've been studying the footage from the camera I left in Kenneth Wilson's bedroom. He hasn't made any move to get rid of his shoes."

A cold wind gusted through my bedroom window.

"Damn. I thought sure we had Bob's killer."

"I don't think so. You may have to accept that Bob's murder was random and his killer may never be caught. However, Ken may kill Tina."

I sucked in a quick breath. "Does that mean you've caught him on tape hurting her?"

As if in answer, lightning struck close by. I shrieked. The flash was so bright it momentarily blinded me, the thunder so loud it hurt my ears.

"You're able to scream," Fred said. "That means the lightning didn't hit you and you're not dead."

"Thank you for being so comforting."

"Any time. Back to Kenneth and Tina. I'm afraid we stirred up Ken with our visit and our talk about Bob. He was rough on her last night. Shouted at her about the affair. Threatened to kill her and the oldest boy, the one that isn't his. Tonight she practically dragged Ken into the bedroom, begging him to hit her instead of the boy, so I assume he must have attacked or at least threatened the kid."

"I don't like the sound of that. Can you turn the video over to the cops and get him arrested?"

"Won't work. If I tried, he'd get me for invasion of his privacy."

"So how were you planning to use the video of him getting rid of his shoes? Wouldn't that have been invasion of privacy too?"

"Absolutely. But if he'd done that, we'd have known he was guilty and then we could have worked on finding the evidence or getting a confession."

"I see. And if he didn't make a move to get rid of the shoes, you could use that as proof to me that he didn't do it and I need to admit that Bob's murder could be an anonymous mugging and quit nagging you about it."

"That sums it up quite well."

"But now you've caught him committing another crime."

"Yes."

"And we can't do anything about it."

"I didn't say that."

Lightning flashed and thunder boomed almost simultaneously. Rain pelted down so suddenly and so hard I jumped. The wind blew chilly drops through my open window and onto my bare arms. I slammed the window closed.

"Go to bed," Fred advised. "Get some sleep. We'll figure out some way to help Tina." He hung up.

I returned to bed, but I didn't expect to sleep. In addition to worrying about Grady, I could now worry about Tina too.

The rain beat against my window so forcefully it seemed it would break the glass and come inside bringing all the cold and darkness that lived outside my house.

Chapter Twelve

The pre-dawn air was cool and rain-cleansed when I left for work the next morning. My front porch held only a few wet leaves blown down by the previous night's turbulence. Nobody jumped out at me when I opened my garage door. Nobody was hiding in the back seat of my car.

I walked into the kitchen of Death by Chocolate to find Paula already at work. Rarely do I arrive before her. Not that I try very hard.

I dropped my purse into a corner of the kitchen and tied on an apron. Making chocolate is a messy process. At least, the way I do it is.

"Good morning." Paula didn't look up from the biscuits she was putting in a pan.

"Somebody sneaked into the hospital and tried to kill Rick again. Failed again."

Her head snapped up, her eyes wide. Yes, I like the effect of being dramatic. "What happened?"

"That's all I know. Trent had to leave in the middle of the night to check on him. And Trent thinks Grady Mathis may be my secret admirer."

She nodded thoughtfully. "Could be. He hits on you every time he comes in here."

I took down a large can of cocoa and began preparing brownies. "Trent's going to talk to him this morning. If he comes in, we need to call Trent immediately."

She shoved the pan of biscuits in the oven and closed the door. "Didn't you get the roses before you even met this guy?"

"Before I went to the car shop, yes. But that place isn't very far from here. Trent thinks he might have been in here prior to that time and I just don't remember him."

"I suppose that's possible. However, he doesn't seem like the kind of man who'd leave romantic gifts like flowers and that butterfly."

"Remember all those romantic gifts Rick used to give me?" I beat my brownie batter vigorously, more vigorously than brownies should be beaten. "Those men don't understand that a few gifts do not make up for how they act."

She set a big bowl of yeast dough in front of me. "Beat on this before you ruin those brownies."

"Speaking of that blasted butterfly, Trent wants it. Good thing because I can't stand having it around if that jerk touched it."

I handed my whisk to Paula and strode into the main room of the restaurant. The butterfly sat quietly on the top shelf of the display case all alone, no cookies to keep it company. Even in the semi-darkness, the crystal wings sparkled. It was pretty even if it was contaminated. It was an inanimate object. Not its fault that a psycho bought it.

Even with all that logic, I still didn't want to touch something Grady Mathis or whoever my stalker was had touched. *Butterflies are free and so are we.* Yuck!

I picked it up using a napkin, took it to the kitchen and set it on top of the refrigerator between my car keys and Paula's so I wouldn't forget it when I left.

৯৯

Breakfast was painful. I couldn't find my rhythm, couldn't get into the zone.

If Grady was my stalker, Trent would put the fear of God and the Pleasant Grove Police Department in him, and that should effectively end the poems, gifts and visits to my house in the middle of the night.

But what if he wasn't?

It could be anyone. The tall man who refused to look me in the eye when he placed his order. The short man who looked me in the eye too long. The skinny man with crossed eyes who might or might not have looked me in the eye.

I poured a cup and a half of coffee for a woman because I was paying more attention to the man at the next table who was writing on his laptop. What was he writing? Was he taking pictures?

Fortunately the coffee didn't spill on the woman, just on the table. "I'm so sorry. I'll get you another cup and be right back to clean that up."

A man at the counter turned as I approached. He had beady, close set eyes.

"Lindsay—"

He knew my name!

"Can I have another cup of Earl Grey?"

Would a stalker drink Earl Grey tea?

I cleaned up the spilled coffee, took the woman another cup, and gave beady eyes hot water and a tea bag.

I tried to pay attention to what I was doing, tried not to be paranoid. However, considering someone was stalking me, spying on me, invading my privacy, paranoia seemed appropriate.

I picked up a fresh pot of coffee. The man walking in the door looked familiar. Tall, dark and handsome, wearing a business suit and an intense expression. Where had I seen him before? Walking down my street? Eating chocolate in my restaurant? Skulking around my house?

Actually, none of those places. The man bore a striking resemblance to Jim Caviezel on *Person of Interest*.

Someone touched my arm. I gasped and almost dropped the coffee pot.

"Why don't you focus on cooking for a while and let me take care of the front room?" Paula asked quietly. "You seem a little distracted."

"I'm fine. I'm not going to allow myself to get upset by some cowardly jerk who sneaks around in the middle of the night and doesn't have the guts to face me."

A woman took a seat at a corner table. Her head was down as if she was studying the empty white mug on the table.

"Excuse me," I said. "I see someone who needs caffeine."

"You know where to find me if you change your mind."

I strode over to the newcomer's table. "Good morning. Can I start you out with a cup of coffee?"

She looked up. It took me a couple of moments to recognize Tina. Both eyes were black, her mouth and cheeks were swollen, and her nose was crooked.

"Holy—!" I bit back the exclamation since there were other customers around who might not appreciate swear words with their breakfast. "Tina? What happened?"

Her unsuccessful attempt to smile lifted one corner of her swollen lips and looked macabre. "You know what happened."

"Well, yes, but shouldn't you be in a hospital or somewhere other than a chocolate shop?"

Tears filled her blood-shot eyes. "I didn't know where else to go. I took the kids to school, went back home and threw a few clothes and toys in the car, then came here. My sister's scared of Ken. She says I can't stay with her. You're so brave, I thought maybe you could help me. You gave me the courage to leave him."

Brave? I've been called a lot of things, some of them not very flattering, but that was the first time I'd ever been called brave. My actions that morning, jumping out of my skin every time a new customer came in, certainly disproved Tina's assumption.

"Uh, okay, sure. What can I do to help?" *Please don't ask me to let you and your three kids stay with me!*

"If I just had a place to stay for a few days until I can find an apartment and get a job, that would help so much."

"There's a Motel 6 not far from here. I understand it's inexpensive but clean and comfortable."

She nodded and tried that strange smile again then looked down at the table. "Could I have a cup of coffee?"

I set the thick white cup upright in its saucer and poured coffee into it.

If she wanted to go to a motel, she wouldn't have come to you. She probably doesn't have the money to pay for even a few nights.

But she has three kids!

Three kids that have to eat.

Three kids!

And motel rooms are very small.

I didn't realize I'd spoken the last thought aloud until Tina said, "We'll be fine at a motel for a few days. I just need to find a place that will let me have all three boys in one room. They're too young to stay by themselves."

"My house is tiny." I gave myself a mental slap upside the head. *Why did I bring up my house?*

"We'll be fine," she repeated.

"My boyfriend's a cop. He probably knows about shelters for abused women where you could stay until you get on your feet."

She still didn't manage much of a smile, but I could see the relieved look in her eyes. "That would be wonderful."

Yes, by that point we all knew Tina and her three sons would be staying at my house *for a few days,* but I wasn't ready to admit it. "How about a hot, gooey cinnamon roll?"

"I'd really like that. I haven't eaten much lately. My stomach's been tied in knots."

"Coming right up."

I went to the kitchen, took my cell phone out of my pocket and called Trent. When he didn't answer, I called Fred. "Can you find me a shelter for abused women?"

"Yes, I can do that. Has Henry been abusing you? I knew that relationship would never work."

"Ha ha. It isn't for me. Remember Tina, Kenneth Wilson's wife? Remember that beating you saw with your hidden camera? I've just seen the results. She's left him."

"Good for her. I have to give her credit. I didn't think she had the courage to do that."

"Yeah, about that. She says I gave her the courage to leave."

"So now you feel responsible for her."

"No, I don't."

He remained silent.

I sighed. "I guess I sort of do. You said yourself our visit probably made things worse for her. Find me a shelter that will take her and her three kids. Please! I'll make you an endless supply of chocolate chip cookies."

"You already do that. I'll get back to you when I find something."

He hung up.

Fred never feels the necessity to say good-bye. He considers it a waste of time.

I took a cinnamon roll to Tina. "Hang tight. You'll have a place to stay before lunch."

Sometimes I have been known to lie.

When the lunch crowd started coming in, my alert ramped to bright red as I studied each man who came in, trying to identify a potential stalker or Tina's abusive husband.

Fred called back shortly after noon. "I've found a shelter that will take Tina and her boys."

I breathed a sigh of relief and went to the kitchen so I could take the call in private. "Thank goodness! Where is it?"

"They will only give the address to Tina. She has to call them and get directions." He gave me a phone number.

I flipped over a business card and wrote the number on it.

"There is a problem, however. They don't have room for them until Sunday."

"Sunday? That's two days away." My voice rose to a high-pitched squeak.

Paula looked up from making a sandwich.

"They can stay in a motel room for two days." Fred didn't have kids. Of course he saw no problem with that scenario.

"No. Find somewhere that can take them now."

"Lindsay, shelters for abused women aren't as commonplace as motels, and they don't have a lot of vacancies. This shelter has a woman and two kids moving out on Saturday, so they'll get Tina in Sunday. That's the best deal I could come up with."

If Fred said it was the best deal, it was the best deal.

Damn!

"What's wrong?" Paula asked.

I slipped my phone back into my jeans pocket. "We can't get Tina and the boys into a shelter until Sunday. There's no space for them."

Paula's gaze locked on mine. "We can't send her back to that man." Her voice was soft, low and urgent.

"Of course not. She can stay in a motel. If she doesn't have the money, I'll pay for it."

Paula's shoulders straightened rigidly and her features took on a determined expression. "She doesn't need to be alone in some cramped, anonymous motel room. She can stay at my house."

If not for the skin around my face, my jaw would have dropped to the floor. "Excuse me? Miss Privacy is inviting a stranger and her three kids to stay in your house?"

"I was a stranger to you, but you helped Zach and me. I don't know if I could have done it without you. The least I can do is pass it on and help another woman and her children."

Paula would do it, take four strangers into her home, but she'd be a nervous wreck. She's come a long way the last couple of years. When I first met her, she grabbed Zach and headed for the safe room when the Avon lady rang the doorbell. Okay, she doesn't have a safe room, but if she had one, she'd have hidden in it for most of that first year.

These days she answers the door when the UPS man comes and even has a male friend (she won't let me call him her boyfriend) who spends time with her. Nevertheless, I was quite certain she wasn't ready for four strangers invading her home for two nights.

I threw up my hands. "Oh, for crying out loud. I'll do it! They can stay at my house. If I survived Rick's mother, his brothers, his ex and his son, I can surely survive Tina and her—" I gulped— "three sons."

Don't get me wrong. I like kids. Well, some kids. I adore Zach. Rick's son, Rickie—not so much. I don't dislike him, but I fervently hope he never comes to stay with me again. I had no idea what Tina's boys were like, but the sheer number of them was intimidating.

"You don't need to do that," Paula said. "I'm okay with letting her stay with Zach and me." She wasn't. I could tell from the determined, terrified look in her eyes.

"We don't have time to argue. We have customers out there who are on the verge of withdrawal from lack of chocolate. Tina's staying with me, and that's that."

I turned on my heel before she could protest and went back to the main room of the restaurant to save all those chocoholics.

The restaurant was packed when Grady Mathis burst in.

His narrowed eyes, grim expression, and the crimson color of his broad face told me Trent had talked to him, but not sternly enough.

He came straight to the cash register where I stood checking out a customer. I refused to let him rattle me though my hand shook slightly as I ran the credit card through the machine.

"Your boyfriend paid me a visit," he bellowed.

The lady whose credit card I held jumped and turned to look at him. A loud silence spread over the room. All conversation and all eating halted in mid-word and mid-bite.

I handed the slip and a pen to the customer and didn't acknowledge Grady's presence. She signed hurriedly and left rapidly.

"I think you should leave," I said quietly.

"Oh, is that right? First some cop tries to tell me what to do and now it's you?" He moved closer to the register and slammed his hand on the counter. "You are one crazy bitch!"

I slid my cell phone from my pocket and hit Trent's speed dial.

Grady grabbed the phone out of my hands, slammed it to the floor and stomped on it then pointed a thick finger at me. "I never done nothing to you! You used me to make that wimpy boyfriend of yours jealous!"

I really hate somebody pointing at me. I grabbed his finger and pushed it up and back.

He screamed, yelled a few words I won't repeat, and withdrew his finger. Mission accomplished.

"Get out of my place." I was surprised my voice came out so calm. I didn't feel calm. I felt angry and scared and...did I mention...angry?

"You think you're so high and mighty, well, let me tell you something, bitch, you're in for a takedown. I tried to be nice to you and then you went and lied on me! You tell that boyfriend of yours he better back off or he'll be sorry! You don't know who you're dealing with, lady."

I grabbed a fork off the counter and thrust it at him. "Get out! Now!"

He laughed, an ugly sound that seemed to come from the oily depths of a sewage dump.

"Lindsay asked you to leave." Paula was suddenly beside me, an industrial size rolling pin clutched in both hands.

Her appearance at my side didn't surprise me, but I was shocked when Tina came up beside Grady. Her bruises stood out from her pale face like dark beacons, and her hand trembled when she held up a cell phone. "I called 911." I could hear the terror in her voice. She was probably having flashbacks of Ken, but she stood her ground. "The police are on their way." Her last words came out in a whisper.

Grady snarled and shoved Tina aside. "I'm going because I can't stand to be in the same room as you, but this isn't over."

He strode toward the door.

"It certainly isn't!" I shouted after him. "You're going to pay for my cell phone!"

Chapter Thirteen

By the time the cops arrived, most of our customers were long gone. As soon as Grady stomped out the door, people began pushing and shoving to pay. Several left without ordering dessert. Those poor folks would spend the rest of the day longing for chocolate. Some might even see imaginary chocolate chips when the CDTs (Chocolate Delirium Tremens) kicked in. I wasn't the only one that jerk harmed.

I didn't recognize either of the officers who responded to Tina's 911 call, but I felt certain they knew Trent. It was a small department. He'd soon hear all about this latest catastrophe. I made it a point to remain calm and dignified in front of them and not mention traffic tickets.

They took statements from me, Paula, Tina and the three customers who remained. I comped the meals for those customers and sent them on their way with extra cookies and brownies. Since Grady had run off so many people before they got a chance to have dessert, I had plenty extra.

The officers left with our statements, my smashed cell phone, and a few cookies. Paula returned to the kitchen, Tina returned to her corner table, and Brandon rushed in the door, eyes wide, face pale. His black eye was fading but still vivid.

174

He ran to where I stood behind the counter and leaned toward me. "Are you all right? The cops wouldn't let me come in. They said it was a crime scene!"

How could Trent have even considered the possibility that this man was involved in some sort of conspiracy with his father? He was as much an innocent victim as I was.

"Your father came in here and made a scene."

He sank onto a stool, held his head in his hands and groaned. "I'm so sorry. It's my fault."

I did not want to hear that. Had Trent been right after all? "Why would you say it's your fault? Your father's nuts." I bit my tongue. Maybe I shouldn't have gone that far. After all, this was his son. "I mean, he's…um…he has a really bad temper."

Brandon lifted his head and smiled. Actually, it was more of a grimace. "Right on both counts. It's my fault because I took you to the shop and introduced you to him."

A chill shot down my spine. "Did he ask you to bring me to the shop?"

Brandon looked genuinely confused. "What? No. I hit your car and offered to fix it for you. Remember?"

"Of course I remember. I just…" I shrugged. "I guess I was looking for an explanation for what your dad did, an explanation for something that doesn't make sense."

Brandon compressed his lips and shook his head. "My dad does a lot of things that don't make sense. He thinks every woman he meets wants to be with

175

him. He cheated on my mother when she was alive, and now that she's dead…" He shrugged and dropped his gaze to the countertop. "I'm sorry."

"Don't worry about it," I said. "But I have to tell you, I'm going to press charges. He destroyed my phone, scared my customers and upset my friends."

"Good. You should press charges. He needs to pay for what he's done." He rose from the stool. "I think I'll skip lunch today. I have some things I have to do."

I laid a restraining hand on his arm. "Please don't confront him. I know you're bigger than he is, but he's mean. He could hurt you."

He gave a snort of laughter. "Believe me, I know that. And I know what I have to do."

I held his arm more tightly. "What is it you have to do?"

He looked down at my hand then back up at me. His smile became almost real. "I'm going to get a place to live. Just like you said I should."

"Good for you! I'm so proud of you!" I released his arm and gave his hand a squeeze. "Let me make you a sandwich to go."

His smile widened. "Thanks."

I went to the kitchen and fixed him a BLT with extra bacon then returned to the counter and threw in a couple of cookies.

"Here you go. Your favorite." I handed the bag to him.

"Thank you." He laid money on the counter. "What happened to your butterfly?"

Did he know his father had left the butterfly? If he didn't, there was no point in fueling his anger. "I put it in the kitchen. I didn't want it to get broken." Two true statements. They had nothing to do with each other, and I shouldn't be faulted if the sequencing made it seem they did. To quote Fred, *I can't help what inference people take from that.*

"Good idea. See you tomorrow." He smiled again and left.

Such a nice guy. Interesting that I had two victims of abuse in my restaurant at the same time. I looked at Tina. She was watching Brandon walk away. Maybe when they were both free of their abusers...

He was a little younger than her, but not enough to matter. I'd have to find out if he liked kids.

A few more customers trickled in, but Grady and the cops had disrupted the busy part of the lunch crowd. Well, I'd have plenty of chocolate to share with Tina's boys. Feed them a pizza, give them some Coke and chocolate, and send them to bed.

If Trent and I ever had kids, I'd have to take a course on how to handle them.

As if conjured from my thoughts, Trent strode in. I delivered a customer's order and rushed to throw myself into his arms. Trent's, not the customer's. Once again I had everybody's attention, but they were all smiling this time.

"I heard what happened," Trent said. "I tried to be tactful when I talked to him, but as soon as I mentioned your name, he went ballistic. This removes any doubt in my mind that he's your stalker. I'm sorry my talk with him made things worse."

I laughed and stepped back. "The tantrum he just threw in here was no worse on my nerves than the disgusting way he usually acts except he threatened you and me both. Said we didn't know who we were dealing with and we'd be sorry. But I think that was just his anger talking." I hoped it was.

"Actually, there's a possibility he could change from adoring stalker to vengeful stalker. But don't worry. We're getting an arrest warrant prepared for creating a public disturbance and destruction of personal property. He should soon be behind bars and then he won't be able to bother you for a while."

"Thank you. Have a seat at the counter and I'll get you something good."

He grinned, a slightly wicked, totally sexy grin.

I punched his arm. "That's for later!" I whispered. "Right now I'm talking about lunch."

"I don't have time. I just came by to give you this." He withdrew a cell phone from his pocket and handed it to me. "I don't want you to be without a phone for even a few hours with that crazy man still on the loose. I picked this up at Wal-Mart. It'll tide you over until you can get a new one." He gave me a quick peck on the cheek. "Gotta get back to work."

"I know. Lock up bad guys. Give speeding tickets to innocent women."

"Don't forget to get those papers from Fred tonight. I'll come over and pick them up and we can talk about that *something good* you promised." His dark eyes twinkled with green.

"About tonight—let me walk you outside." I took his arm and led him out the front door.

"What's up?" He turned to look through the plate glass windows into the restaurant. "Who are we avoiding?"

I put a big, phony smile on my face. "Stop frowning! She'll see you!"

"Who?"

"Tina. The lady in the corner booth."

"The one staring down at her empty plate? I don't think she's going to see anything except a crumb or two."

I told him about Tina's situation. "Fred found her a place at one of the shelters starting Sunday, but she's spending Friday and Saturday night at my place."

"Oh." The green sparks disappeared from his eyes. He was so uptight, he wouldn't spend the night with me if someone else was there. "Lindsay, you've got a good heart, but sometimes I wonder about your head."

"Yeah, right. What else was I supposed to do? I couldn't let her go back to Ken, and I don't think she has the money for a motel room. It's only for two nights. Maybe Saturday I can come to your place."

"We can definitely do that, but I was thinking about the danger you're putting yourself in. Abusive husbands don't like it when their wives escape. If Tina's husband comes after her, you could be collateral damage. So now I've got to worry about Grady Mathis and Ken Wilson. I'll be over tonight anyway and sleep on the sofa."

"Well, no, that's not going to work. Tina has three sons. That takes care of my guest bed, the sofa and Fred's inflatable mattress."

He scowled and ran a hand through his already messy hair. "I've got to go, but this discussion is not over. I'll be there tonight."

We exchanged a brief kiss and he left.

I hadn't thought about Ken coming after Tina. I didn't see any way he could find her at my place. Fred had not given him our last names or told him where we lived. But he had mentioned that Bob was murdered in the alley behind a restaurant where a friend of his worked. It wouldn't take a lot of brain power to figure out from the news reports that the restaurant in question was Death by Chocolate.

I had told Tina in private that I was the owner. Surely she hadn't mentioned anything to Ken, and he hadn't seemed smart enough or sober enough to make a connection. Nevertheless, I wouldn't give Henry much catnip while Tina was staying with me. He needed to be alert.

When I got back inside, Paula was checking out the last customer. As soon as he left, I started to lock the door but Tina stopped me. "I need to leave. I have to pick up my kids at school. Will you still be here when I get back?"

"Of course," I assured her. "We have to clean up. We'll be here another couple of hours. If you don't see us, just bang on the door."

Tina reached for the door handle.

"What if Ken's at the school?" Paula asked.

Tina turned back and licked her lips. Her pupils shrank to pinpoints. "I—I don't think he knows we're gone yet. He hasn't called. He won't get home from work for another couple of hours."

Paula moved closer. "He'll recognize your car before you have a chance to get them. You can take mine. It's parked out back."

Tina blinked a couple of times in rapid succession. So did I. Paula seemed determined to help this woman who was in a situation she knew too well.

"No, I couldn't," Tina said.

"Yes, you can," Paula insisted. "Even if you think he won't be at the school, you can't be sure. Abusive men are sneaky and clever. Take the car. Keep yourself and your boys safe."

Paula led her to the kitchen. I followed with the last of the dirty dishes.

Paula's short so when she reached for her keys on the top of the refrigerator, she didn't see the butterfly. As she retrieved her keys, the crystal slid from the top of the refrigerator. We all three grabbed for it. Tina had the quickest reaction. Probably came from years of dodging her husband's fists.

She held the object reverently in both hands. "It's so beautiful. I'm glad it didn't break."

She offered it to me. I flinched away from it. She turned to Paula who shook her head. "It's Lindsay's."

Lindsay's bane. "Maybe you could do me a favor. I need to take it home tonight to give to Trent, but I've got so many other things to carry, I'm afraid I'll forget it. Could you take it with you?"

She smiled. "I'd love to. It will be nice to have something pleasant to focus on instead of...well, you know. I promise I'll keep it safe."

The two of them went out the back door and I returned to dirty dishes and my thoughts. Both Paula and Trent seemed to think Kenneth Wilson had super powers. I figured he had a room temperature IQ, and we're talking about an air conditioned room in the middle of winter. But maybe they knew something I didn't about the abilities of abusive men.

Even though I couldn't imagine that Ken Wilson could find Tina at my house, I would let her park her car in my garage just to be on the safe side.

❧❧

Tina made the kid pickup without incident. She and Paula exchanged cars again, then Tina followed me home while Paula went to get Zach from the babysitter.

My first encounter with the boys was at my house. Tina and I both parked at the curb. I got out and started toward her to tell her to put her car in my garage but halted in mid-stride when three car doors on Tina's battered sedan flew open. Three boys in blue jeans and T-shirts burst forth, shouting, chattering, pushing and shoving.

Tina slid out of the driver's seat. "Boys, be quiet." She was only a couple of inches taller than the oldest one, but they obeyed her. "Lindsay Powell, this is Wade, Connor and Drake." She pointed to the boys in order of size.

They all mumbled some version of *Nice to meet you, Ms. Powell*.

182

"Hi, Wade, Connor and Drake. Tina, why don't you pull up in the driveway and we'll put your car in the garage."

She considered that suggestion only a moment before nodding and getting back in her car.

"Wow, Mom gets to use the garage!" Wade exclaimed. "Dad never lets her use the garage."

"That's because Mom's car's old and ugly," Drake said.

It was.

I pulled into the driveway behind Tina then got out and opened the door to the garage. She drove inside.

The boys were right there.

"Your garage is falling down," Connor said.

Drake stepped closer to peer inside. "You don't have a motorcycle."

"Dad's going to let me ride his motorcycle when I'm twelve," Wade said proudly.

Tina came out of the garage carrying two suitcases and gave me a *No, he isn't* look. Ken might be a bully, but I sensed that Tina was in charge of the kids—as much as anybody is in charge of kids, especially when they come in packs.

I took one of her suitcases, grabbed the bag of leftovers, and we crossed the yard to the house. The boys darted around us, eager to explore their new surroundings.

I opened the front door and, as expected, King Henry waited just inside. But he didn't step out to wind around my legs or give me a homecoming head butt as he usually does. He surveyed the group behind me, tilted his head arrogantly, hefted his tail into the air and trotted toward the kitchen.

"Welcome to my home." I stepped inside and held the door to invite the others in.

Tina came in with her suitcases, and all three boys tried to come through the door at once. After much scrambling and shouting, they managed to get in and I locked the door behind them.

A cell phone rang. It was a generic sound, not the wind chimes tone I had my phone set to, but I didn't have my phone anymore. I put my bag of goodies on the coffee table and reached for the burner phone in my pocket.

Tina held hers in her hand and stared at it as the ringing continued. I peeked over her shoulder. A picture of Ken Wilson along with his first name showed on the screen.

Oh boy. The fun begins.

"Can we turn on the TV?" one of the boys shouted.

"Sure, go ahead." What was one more source of noise?

Tina continued to stare at her phone which continued to ring. "Should I answer it?" Her quiet words trembled and hung in the air.

"Uh…" I had no idea what to tell her. She needed Paula's advice, not mine. Sometimes I answered Rick's calls and sometimes I ignored them. "If you want to talk to him, answer. If you don't, ignore it." That was the best advice I could come up with.

She looked at me with a terrified expression. "I don't want to talk to him."

"Don't answer."

"He'll keep calling."

"Keep not answering."

She bit her swollen lip. "Would you mind if I kept the kids inside this evening instead of letting them play in the yard? I just worry about Ken somehow finding us."

I nodded, recalling Paula's protective attitude toward Zach. It was better now, but she still worried. Of course Tina would worry about her sons.

Underneath the shouts of the kids and the roar of the television, I distinctly heard the sound of a hungry tiger in my kitchen. Okay, a distant relative of a tiger, but he sounded upset.

"Excuse me. I have to feed my cat." *And get away from the bedlam.*

"Get your feet off the sofa and sit up straight."

I was pretty sure Tina wasn't talking to me so I kept going.

When I first moved into the house, a door separated the kitchen and the living room. I like open spaces. That door currently resides in the garage. I wondered briefly how long it would take me to put it up again.

Henry looked into his empty bowl then up at me accusingly.

"Chill out. You're not going to starve."

He continued to focus his ice blue stare on me. He didn't believe me.

Sally Berneathy

I poured nuggets in his bowl and added some stinky, fishy mixture from a can. He needed to be fortified to face the evening.

"Mama, he hit me!"

"Did not!"

"Sit down and be quiet, all of you." Tina's voice.

I couldn't tell if they sat down but they didn't stop shouting.

About half the stinky, fishy mixture remained in the can. I raked it all into Henry's bowl then watched him eat. No, I don't usually stand and watch my cat eat but I wasn't ready to go back into the melee. Tina's boys didn't seem as bent on destruction and disobedience as Rick's son had been, but they weren't quiet and sweet like Zach either. I wondered if Zach would turn into a wild boy in the next three years.

Probably.

I tossed the cat food can into the trash and opened the refrigerator door. Coke or wine? It was only five thirty, but the evenings were growing shorter with the approach of winter. A shorter evening justified an earlier first drink.

"Why haven't you answered your phone?"

I gasped and spun around to see Fred standing in my kitchen doorway. He was immaculate as always, every white hair in place, knit shirt and blue jeans unwrinkled, black framed glasses free of spots. Nevertheless he had a disheveled look about him. Running the obstacle course that existed in my living room would have that effect.

186

"Are you talking about my land line? I just got home. I guess I didn't hear it ring over all the noise."

"No, your cell phone. I've left eleven messages. I was getting ready to call Trent when you drove up with your new roommates."

"Oh, my cell phone. I don't have that anymore. Grady Mathis came into the shop today, yelled at me and stomped on my cell phone."

Behind his sparkling lenses Fred's eyes widened. He swallowed, his Adam's apple lifting and plunging with the action. "Lindsay, we need to talk about him."

"It's okay. He won't bother me again. The cops are going to arrest him for creating a public disturbance, destroying my property, and just generally being a disgusting excuse for a human being."

"That's good news. Is Trent coming over tonight?"

"Yes. He wants to get that box and wrapping paper from you that the butterfly came in."

"That's what I wanted to talk to you about. I believe Grady is Rick's attacker. I found Rick's blood on the wrapping paper."

Chapter Fourteen

I stumbled to the table, pulled out a chair and sank into it. "You mean...?" I couldn't say it. I was having a hard time wrapping my brain around the implications of what Fred had just told me.

He sat in a chair next to me. "I mean your secret admirer tried to kill your ex-husband." Fred doesn't believe in wasting anything, not even words.

I opened my mouth but only one syllable came out. "Coke."

"Lindsay, did you just croak?" Sophie stood in the kitchen doorway. She wore a white cotton blouse that set off her dark hair perfectly, and she looked totally composed. Had she come up from the basement through a hidden trap door I didn't know about or down through the roof? She could not possibly look that serene after coming through the fracas going on in my living room.

Fred unfolded himself from his chair and sauntered to the refrigerator. "She needs a fix." He took out a cold Coke, popped the top and brought it to me. "Did you bring home any chocolate? I think you need some before we go on."

"It's in a bag on the coffee table."

"I'll get it." Sophie started to the living room.

"Don't go in there!" I warned.

She turned back. "Why not?"

Really? Had she gone deaf?

"Give that back! It's mine!" Drake shouted.

"Is not!" Wade declared.

"Mama!"

"Wade, take this car and leave your brother alone."

"Don't move a muscle or I'll shoot!"

I was pretty sure that last came from the TV. I fervently hoped it came from the TV.

Apparently my idea that Tina was in control of her sons had been naïve.

"Sophie, there are kids in there," I said. "Lots of kids."

"I know. Aren't children adorable?"

I looked at Fred to see how he was taking that comment. He doesn't do well around kids. Or cats. Or dust mites. Or dust.

He sat down again, looking completely unconcerned. Either he really was unconcerned or he was pretending.

Sophie smiled and disappeared into the chaos.

"Do you think she'll make it back alive?"

"Don't worry about Sophie. She's stronger than she looks."

"How do you know that?"

He scowled. "How do you *not* know that?"

Fred would have made a good politician. For all I knew, that might be on his resume.

"Lindsay, there's a possibility Grady killed Ginger." His voice was calm and quiet, and it took a couple of seconds for his words to register.

I blinked a few times, forcing my mind back to a place it didn't want to go. "Uh...what?"

"If we assume Grady tried to kill Rick then rushed to your house to leave a gift, we can assume he was trying to help you by killing someone who caused you problems."

"We can?"

"It fits the pattern."

"It does? What pattern?"

"The pattern of being obsessed with someone, bringing gifts, doing what the stalker considers good deeds to win the love of the object of his obsession."

"How would he know about Rickhead? Yeah, I complain about him a lot, but I'm sure I never complained to Grady." I wrapped my arms around myself and shuddered. "I have never shared anything personal with that creep."

"From the content of his poems, we know he's been watching you. He may have been monitoring your activities for some time. He could have seen Ginger when she came to your house in the middle of the night. He could have witnessed Rick's rampage in your restaurant. With all the electronic devices available, he could have listened to your conversations at home and at work. He could have watched you through your windows at night."

Thinking of that awful, creepy, disgusting man watching from the street was bad enough, but the thought of him watching me eating, sleeping, and talking on the phone slid over my skin like spiders and put a bad taste in my mouth. I tried to wash it out with Coke, but it even made the Coke taste bitter.

Sophie returned to the kitchen and set my bag of goodies on the table then sank gracefully into a chair beside Fred.

I opened the bag and drew out a brownie but stopped before shoving it into my mouth. "It's full. All the cookies and brownies are still here."

Sophie nodded. "Tina told the boys they couldn't have any until after dinner. They're such good kids."

"You can't kill me!" Connor shouted. "I'm a zombie!"

"I'm a werewolf and I'm gonna eat you all up!" Drake threatened.

I bit into the brownie, hoping the taste of rich chocolate would overpower the sour taste of Grady watching me as well as the noise of those good kids in the other room.

But not even chocolate could cover the bile from the thought of that man. I choked down the bite in my mouth and set the rest on the table.

"Are you okay?" Sophie asked.

"No. Not even close." I swallowed then licked my dry lips. I did not want to voice my fears, hear them spoken aloud and let them escape into the universe with the great and terrible power of words.

Sophie laid a hand over mine. "None of this is your fault. You can't blame yourself for what a mad man did."

Apparently I was the last to know murder had been committed in my name. I tried another drink of Coke. It was flat, all the happy bubbles gone.

"I believe we're dealing with a very dangerous man, a psychopath who's lost all touch with reality," Fred said.

"And I fed that psychopath chocolate in my restaurant." I shivered as those spiders made another trip across my skin. "I'm glad he's going to be behind bars soon. I wouldn't sleep a wink tonight if I thought he was still out there."

Fred drew in a deep breath. He was getting ready to say something I wasn't going to like. "I think it would be a good idea if I spent the night over here."

Everybody thinking I needed a bodyguard was getting a little old. "Sure," I said. "Sounds like a great idea. Would you like to share the sofa with Tina or the guest bed with the boys?"

"Actually, I thought I could bring over an air mattress and sleep in front of the door."

"I was planning to borrow that air mattress for one of the boys."

"I have more than one air mattress. I'll bring two."

"You're being silly. By now Trent has arrested Grady and hauled him off to jail. Anyway, Tina's going to be sleeping on the sofa, and your snoring would keep her awake."

"I don't snore."

I looked at Sophie to see how she'd react, if she'd affirm or deny his assertion. She was nibbling on a cookie without getting crumbs on the table.

"Trent volunteered to spend the night here, and I'm going to tell him he can." Sure, it was a lie, but it was such an absurd lie, nobody would believe it. That

192

kind of lie doesn't count in the negative column in the karmic realm governing truths and lies.

"And he'll be happy to take you up on that." A familiar voice came from the kitchen doorway.

Busted.

Trent took the remaining chair at the table between Sophie and me.

"You were eavesdropping," I accused.

"It's still admissible in court. I even have two witnesses who also heard you say you're going to let me spend the night here."

I shrugged. "As long as you sleep in my bed, that's fine."

"We'll borrow both of Fred's air mattresses. The third boy in your guest room can use one, and Tina can sleep on the other in the upstairs bedroom where you keep your computer. I'll sleep on the sofa near the door."

I stood. "That's ridiculous. There's no way Ken can find my house, and with Grady in jail and Rick in the hospital, I'm safe. Speaking of dirt bags, Fred has something to tell you about Grady. I believe we've solved a couple of crimes for you." Perhaps *we* was stretching it a bit, but I deserved a little credit since I was the psycho's focus. "In the meantime, I'm going to order pizzas. Feed the zombies and werewolves."

I took my cell phone from my pocket, moved to one side of the kitchen and placed the order while Fred and Trent talked. The din from the living room had become so loud, I could barely hear the pizza people. Fortunately I ordered pizza so often, I knew what the questions were and could respond even when I couldn't make out the words. I couldn't make out what Fred and Trent were saying either.

I grabbed four cans of Coke and a stack of paper plates then ventured into the living room. Surely they'd be quiet while they were guzzling Coke and anticipating pizza.

Tina sat on the sofa with her cell phone in her hand and a dazed expression on her face. The boys were taking full advantage of her virtual absence to wreak havoc. Fortunately I didn't have anything breakable in the room, but they'd used all the books from my bookcase to make a fort that didn't survive an assault from enemy forces. Or maybe it was friendly fire. Hard to tell in the melee.

Drake crouched under the coffee table and growled while Wade and Connor charged around the room, shouting, jumping over the table, onto the sofa and off the back of the sofa. It was a very durable sofa.

Henry pressed against my leg and I realized he'd followed me from the kitchen. I looked down at him. He looked up at me, flattened his ears and skirted around the room, hugging the wall, pausing only long enough to hiss when somebody darted close. He reached the stairs and flowed upward in a streak of white and gold.

I looked for the remote control to turn off the TV and stop some of the noise, but I didn't see it. Probably another casualty of the war. I walked over to the set and pressed a button, effectively silencing a lizard with an ambiguous accent who was trying to sell us insurance. The boys continued their shouting and mayhem and Tina continued to stare at her phone.

I crossed to the sofa, skirting the coffee table and the werewolf holding siege under it while two zombies attacked. Connor wielded the remote like a sword.

I set the unopened Cokes on top of the werewolf's cave and sank down next to Tina. She must have turned off her ring tone because her phone was silent though a call was coming in from *Ken*.

"He's calling nonstop now." She spoke softly without lifting her head. "He's filled up my voice mail."

"That doesn't sound good. Have you listened to any of the messages?"

She nodded. "His first message was sweet. I almost caved. He said he was getting worried because the kids and I weren't home. He wanted to know if I needed help. Then he must have checked the bedrooms and found the missing clothes and suitcases because he started leaving mean, horrible messages, calling me names and saying things like how I'm his wife and I have no right to do this and he's going to make me pay when he finds me."

"Don't worry. We've got a cop and a..." I paused, unsure how to describe Fred. A spy? A hired assassin? Black ops? "A cop and a man who does Karate and owns a machine gun."

She turned the phone over and laid it on the cushion beside her, hiding Ken's face from view. "Thank you for everything. I know that the boys and I are safe here, but I'm still terrified he'll find us."

"He'll be sorry if he does."

She placed a hand over the phone, hiding it from view. "Even if I don't talk to him or listen to his messages, he's still in my head. The physical abuse is only part of it. I keep hearing all the terrible things he constantly says to me, how I'm worthless and not a good mother and could never make it without him and any other man would leave me and..." She paused and forced a smile. "I know I have to get away from him, but I don't know if I can."

"Yes, you can. I'll call Paula. She'll come over and talk to you. She's been through this." I took my cell phone from my pocket.

Tina lifted hers from the sofa. "I'm going to erase all those horrible voice mails he left."

"No! We need those as evidence."

"Evidence?"

"Monday we're going to call the lawyer who handled my divorce. He'll file divorce papers for you."

Her eyes widened.

"Okay, maybe we'll start with a legal separation and an order of protection." As the daughter of a lawyer I knew how much good those restraining orders did. Usually it was like waving a red flag in front of an enraged bull. But maybe the process would give Tina more courage.

She swallowed, blinked and finally nodded. "Okay."

I had to wonder if she was so accustomed to taking orders from Ken, she'd agree to anything I told her to do. That was not necessarily a bad thing as long as I was telling her what to do, not Ken.

I called Paula and she came over immediately.

I expected Zach to be intimidated by the loud, boisterous boys the way he'd been intimidated by sly, sneaky Rickie. To my shock and horror, when the boys invited him to play with them, he dashed over and began jumping and shouting along with them.

Paula gave me an *OMG, what have you done to my son?* look.

I couldn't stand it any longer. I had already sustained as much permanent hearing damage as if I'd sat next to a speaker at twenty rock concerts with no ear protection. "Stop!" I screamed and was answered with a moment of beautiful silence.

But only a moment.

"Boys!" Tina shouted. "Settle down."

"Yes, Mama," Wade mumbled.

"Okay," Drake said quietly.

Then they all started giggling and I could foresee that the sound level would soon rise again.

The doorbell rang.

Tina froze. So did I.

Paula walked over and looked through the peephole then opened the door. The pizza delivery boy stood on my front porch. I dared to breathe again. The kids began shouting again.

"Yay, pizza!" Connor jumped up and down.

"I love pizza!" Drake jumped higher.

"Pizza, pizza, pizza!" The last came from Zach. Surely this was a temporary break with reality and he would return to being a quiet only child when he got home. I certainly hoped so, or I'd be in a world of trouble with Paula.

I set two pizzas on the coffee table and took the other one into the kitchen. Trent, Fred and Sophie looked up as I entered. The guilty expressions on all three faces told me they'd been talking about me. Usually I consider it better to be talked about than forgotten, but I had a feeling they hadn't been saying anything I wanted to hear.

I put the pizza in the middle of the table and was about to demand to know what they'd been talking about, but Paula came in.

"Can I get some juice for Zach?"

"Sure." I filled a sippy cup with cranberry juice and handed it to her then reached back into the refrigerator and got a bottle of wine. "You and Tina are going to need this." I opened the wine and took two glasses from the cabinet.

"Thank you." She accepted the bottle without hesitation. "It would be great if you could corral the kids in here after they eat. Tina and I have a lot to talk about."

I looked around the small room. No freaking way. "Okay, sure." I took another bottle of wine out of the refrigerator and opened it. "One adult to one child. We can do that. I get Zach."

She smiled and left the room, juggling the wine, glasses and juice with the expertise I'd often seen her display at Death by Chocolate.

I got more glasses and paper plates then sat down at the table.

Everyone was very quiet. I could understand that. My nerves were shattered like a plate glass window when someone throws a brass candle stick through it. Never mind how I know that.

"Enjoy," I said. "We're going to need sustenance if we have to babysit the kids. Notice I said *we*, so don't think any of you are going to escape."

I opened the box and took out a slice of pepperoni pizza.

Fred poured wine into a glass and handed it to me. He and everyone else looked grim. I decided I didn't want to know what they'd been talking about when I was out of the room.

I wiped the string of cheese off my chin and stared at the three solemn faces. "Hey, I was kidding. If you don't want to babysit the kids while Paula talks to Tina, go home. I can handle it. I'll just give them some ice cream with Benadryl syrup."

Nobody smiled. My fabled humor was not working as a diversion.

"Kidding again. I don't even have any Benadryl syrup. I'll have to crush some tablets."

Trent took my hand and looked into my eyes. This was getting scary.

I returned his gaze. "If you're getting ready to tell me you had the mumps as a boy and you'll never father any children, I'm okay with that."

"Fred and I are both spending the night with you," he said.

"Well, all right, but you're sleeping in the middle. I have to get up to go to the bathroom sometimes."

199

"This isn't a joke. Fred told me about Rick's blood on the wrapping paper and his suspicions about Ginger's death."

"But you arrested Grady." I gulped and slowly lowered my pizza to my paper plate. "Didn't you?"

"We went to his business and his home. We couldn't find him at either place. Lindsay, Grady Mathis is free and probably very angry at you right now."

Chapter Fifteen

My house is old. It was built at a time when an indoor bathroom was considered a luxury. Only the very rich had more than one. That's how I started Saturday morning in the same bathroom as Wade, Connor and Drake.

They didn't all come in at the same time. It took them a while to congregate. I was in the shower washing my hair when Drake opened the door and yelled, "I gotta pee!"

"I'll be out in a few minutes!"

Silly me. I thought he'd leave when he knew the bathroom was occupied. I realized my mistake when the toilet flushed and my warm shower became scalding acid. I screamed and turned off the water.

"Drake!" Wade shouted. "You're not supposed to go in the bathroom while the lady's in there! Get out of there!"

Thank goodness one of them had some knowledge of bathroom etiquette!

"I gotta wash my hands. Mama says I always gotta wash my hands."

"Is it time to get up?" Connor joined the crowd.

"We're sorry, Mrs. Powell," Wade said.

"It's *Miss*," I corrected automatically.

"Yeah," Connor shouted, "he missed! Drake, you dumb butt, you peed on the floor!"

"Did not! I'm gonna tell Mama you said *butt*!"

"Get some toilet paper and clean it up, Drake," Wade ordered.

"It's okay." I huddled behind my shower curtain with conditioner in my hair, beginning to shiver as the sensation of being boiled alive wore off. "I'll do it."

"Mama says if we make a mess, we gotta clean it up," Wade said.

"I understand that would usually apply, but this is my bathroom." At least, it was yesterday morning. "I'll do it."

"That's too much paper, you dummy." Connor again. "Hurry up. I gotta pee really bad."

"You can't do it while Drake's cleaning the floor."

"How about, *you can't do it while I'm taking a shower?*"

"He's almost done."

I had no idea if Wade was talking about Drake or Connor.

"Wash your hands again," Wade ordered.

Must be Drake. Connor hadn't washed his hands yet this morning. That I knew of. But I'd lost track of all the events going on in my own bathroom some time ago.

"What are you boys doing up so early?" Tina. Thank goodness.

"Drake peed on the floor," Wade said.

"Did not! It was just a dribble."

I heard the sound of running water. "This is how you do it. See? I'm not peeing on the floor," Connor bragged.

"Be quiet and get back to bed," Tina ordered. "You're going to wake up Lindsay!"

"Lindsay's very much awake," I called from the shower.

"Omigawd! You went in the bathroom while Lindsay's in the shower? Get back to bed right now, all of you! I am so sorry, Lindsay."

"Oh, no problem." My hair should be really smooth and shiny after leaving the conditioner on so long. I turned the water back on and shivered while it warmed up.

"You know better than that." Tina sounded angry. "If your daddy was here..." She stopped in mid-sentence as if she'd suddenly realized what she was saying and didn't want to remind them of the man she was running from.

"But Daddy's not here," Wade reminded her quietly. He sounded relieved.

I hoped his statement would remain true.

"The boys are going back to their room," Tina said. "I'm going to close the bathroom door so you can shower in peace. Again, I'm so sorry."

I finished my shower, put on my robe and headed back to my room. The door to the guest room was closed. Inside the boys were giggling and talking. Weren't kids supposed to sleep late on Saturday morning, get up about noon and watch cartoons?

I dressed, and Henry and I went downstairs.

Trent was asleep on the sofa. He looked adorable lying there in his rumpled clothes, his feet hanging off one end, his mouth slightly open, snoring softly.

Henry nudged my leg and darted toward the kitchen. His breakfast could not be delayed.

I tiptoed into the kitchen and saw Fred lying on his air mattress in front of the back door. He appeared to be sleeping. I moved closer to finally answer the question of whether Fred ever slept. His breathing was slow and even and he wasn't wearing his glasses. I was certain I'd caught him sleeping.

His eyes opened.

I gasped and jumped back.

He sat up and frowned. "What's wrong with you?"

"Nothing. I've got to feed Henry."

I poured food into the bowl while Fred let the air out of his mattress.

He folded it with such precision it fit into the bag it came in. Magical powers.

I returned to the living room where Trent still slept, leaned over to kiss his forehead then moved my lips to his ear to whisper something I found difficult to say while he was awake. This would be good practice for the awake part.

"I'm going to walk you to your car and follow you to work." Fred was right behind me.

I straightened and looked at him. Whatever he'd been doing on that air mattress all night didn't involve rumpling his clothes. They were probably made from special fabric from the planet Krypton. He was wearing his glasses again, his disguise as a mild-mannered neighbor back in place.

"Me too." Trent's voice was raspy with sleep.

I turned to find him sitting up, rubbing his eyes. "You too what? You don't even know what we're talking about. Go back to sleep. It's still dark outside."

"Me too, I'm walking you to your car and then I'm going to drive behind you to work and make sure you get inside safely."

I arched an eyebrow. "You really think you can keep up with me? I'll be halfway to the restaurant before you wake up enough to figure out where my front door is."

Behind me Fred snorted. "I'll give you a five minute handicap while I get my car."

I sighed, resigning myself to having an escort.

I would never admit it to them, but I was actually a little relieved they were going with me. Grady could be waiting on my front porch or in the alley behind Death by Chocolate. Ken could have tracked down Tina. Evil could be lurking in the darkness.

I made the journey to Death by Chocolate with Trent in the lead and Fred on my bumper. We all parked behind the restaurant and got out.

"Paula's here. The lights are on inside and that's her car," I said. "You can go home now."

Trent took my arm. "As soon as we're sure Paula's the only one here."

I rolled my eyes, but again I was secretly a little relieved. I didn't want to walk into the restaurant and find Paula tied to a chair while Grady boiled a chocolate rabbit on the stove.

Paula looked up in surprise when we entered. She was alone, unfettered, rolling out dough as usual. "Good morning. I haven't started the coffee yet, but I can put some on. It'll be ready in a few minutes."

"Thanks, but we can't stay," Trent said. "We wanted to be sure Lindsay got here safely."

Paula shuddered. "I hope you find Grady and arrest him today."

"Fred and I are going to be working on that," he assured her.

Two of the three important men in my life (Henry's the third) don't always get along. Trent doesn't approve of Fred's methods and Fred…well, he's Fred. I was glad they would be working together. I was certain Grady had no chance to escape with the two of them after him.

"Thanks for the escort," I said.

Trent gave me a quick kiss on the cheek, and the two of them left. I closed then locked the door, something I don't usually do. But there isn't usually a psycho murderer stalking me.

"It took me half an hour and two glasses of milk to get Zach calmed down last night," Paula said. "How much longer will your guests be there?"

"They leave tomorrow."

She nodded. "I suppose we can get through one more evening."

"Maybe you can. I'm not sure I can." I told her about the bathroom scene. It was, I thought, rather rude of her to laugh.

❧❧

We open late on Saturday and only serve brunch so it's a short day. However, the three hours we served customers stretched to eternity. Every time the bell over the front door jingled, my heart stopped until I saw it wasn't Grady coming in.

Finally the day was over and we put up the closed sign.

Then a new terror hit me.

Only a couple of hours until I had to go home and face the Hyper Horde. Only a couple of hours until my peace and eardrums would be shattered.

"What are you doing?" Paula asked as I moved the broom across the floor in slow motion.

"I think I'll just spend the night here."

"You can't do that. You have to go home and rescue Henry."

I groaned and swept a little faster. Henry knew how to hide, but he did need me to get his food out of the pantry.

Trent called as Paula and I were finishing our cleanup.

"Did you catch him?" First words out of my mouth. Damn! That wasn't what I'd intended to say. So much for pretending to be nonchalant and unconcerned.

A moment of silence followed, a poignant silence if I've ever heard one. "Not yet. I'm having trouble getting a search warrant for his house and place of business. My lab won't even look at the DNA on that wrapping paper. Fred broke the official chain of custody." He might be working with Fred, but his words were saturated with disapproval of Fred's methods.

"It's not his fault. I was going to throw it away, give it to Henry to destroy, burn it and flush it down the toilet stool."

"I know. Fred did the best possible thing under the circumstances. I just wish you'd reported those gifts to us in the first place."

"I thought they were from Rickhead!"

"I'm not getting on your case." He sighed. I could almost see him running his fingers through his hair in frustration. "I'm just worried. Does Grady's son still come in for lunch?"

"He was here yesterday, but I haven't seen him today."

"He lives with his dad, right?"

"Yes." I'd been so distracted by Tina's kids and the threat of Grady still out there, I hadn't thought about Brandon. Suddenly the pieces of the puzzle slammed into place and created a terrifying picture. "Oh, no! Their shop was closed and nobody answered the door at their home? Where's Brandon? I hope Grady didn't do something to him! He gave him a black eye a few days ago. I knew I shouldn't have told Brandon about that scene his dad made in the restaurant. Brandon was really upset. What if he confronted his father and…?" I couldn't finish the *what if*.

"Don't jump to conclusions. He probably went to stay with friends, maybe a girlfriend."

I sucked in a deep breath and tried to calm my frantic mind. "Maybe. He hasn't mentioned a girlfriend, but he's been looking for a place to live so he can get away from his dad. Maybe he does have someone."

"Do you know how to contact him? If he lives and works with his father, he can give us permission to search the house and business without a warrant."

"He gave me his business card and wrote his cell number on the back. I'll look for it when I get home."

"Call me when you leave the restaurant, and this one time I'll let you talk on your cell phone and drive at the same time."

He really was worried.

೯೦ ೩೦

For once I drove home slowly, drawing out the conversation with Trent and lingering as long as I could before confronting the very energetic children in my house. I had a large bag of chocolate goodies in the passenger seat that I planned to use to bribe the kids into silence or, failing that, glue their mouths shut with gooey peanut butter bars.

As I pulled into my drive, I was pleased to see the house was still standing.

"Signing off," I said. "Nobody in the yard."

"You don't hang up until you're inside."

I got out of my car and headed across the yard. Nobody jumped out from behind the oak tree. Nobody lurked around the side of the house. Of course, it was three thirty in the afternoon. Most lurking occurs after dark.

"I need to buy a gun. Then you and Fred wouldn't have to worry about me."

"You and a gun in the same room? I'd really worry about you then."

"Stepping onto the porch and all is well." I heard noises from inside, but I couldn't see anything. Tina had left the blinds closed, presumably so Ken couldn't see in if he found her. I knew the odds of him finding her at my house were small, but *small* isn't the same thing as zero.

A white flash shot out of the bushes and onto the porch. Henry looked up at me with a pitiful expression. "And my guard cat's here. All is well. I'm coming to your house to spend the night, right?"

"Right. I'll bring burgers and rings for everybody, and you can come home with me after we eat. We can even take Henry if you want."

"He'll be fine as long as I get home early tomorrow morning to feed him."

"I've got a couple of things to do, but I'll see you around seven thirty or eight. Love you, babe."

"Me too." Okay, I didn't actually say the words, but just the *me too* was a big step for Rickhead's ex-wife. After that nightmare of betrayal, it was hard to open up and expose myself again.

I put my cell phone in my pocket and unlocked the door. "Have you been hiding outside all day?" I asked Henry.

He meowed and stayed behind me as we went in. I've seen him take down a large dog without even breathing hard, but Tina's kids had him cowering. I felt the same way. Not that I've taken down any large dogs.

"Hi, Mrs. Powell!" Connor shouted from his perch astride the back of my sofa.

"Connor, get down from there!" Tina rushed in from the kitchen, her blond hair straggling from a ponytail, an exhausted expression on her face. She hit the button on the TV and the noise level fell significantly. "Oh, Drake, I can't leave you alone for a minute! Don't worry, Lindsay, I have a great formula for getting magic marker off your walls. Wade? Where are you, Wade?" She looked frantically around the room.

Wade slid down the banister. "I like this house!"

"Young man, get over here this minute! You are not to leave this room!" She pushed a few strands of hair off her face and turned to me. "I'm sorry, Lindsay. They're usually better behaved than this."

"I want to play outside!" Connor bounced off the sofa and landed in front of his mother.

"You can't play outside. Maybe tomorrow when we get to our new home."

I wasn't sure I could survive until tomorrow. Henry remained behind me, not even demanding his food. His ears lay flat against his head, and his tail stood rigidly in the air.

"Drake! No!" Tina caught her youngest son's arm just as he was about to launch the infamous crystal butterfly across the room.

"I want to see the butterfly fly!" His mouth turned down in a pout.

"You dummy!" Wade planted himself in front of Drake, hands on his hips. "That's not a real butterfly. It'll break if you throw it!"

"Mama, Wade called me a dummy!"

"That's enough, Wade. He didn't mean it, Drake. But he's right that you'll break this butterfly if you throw it. This belongs to Miss Powell. She'll be very upset if you break it."

I wouldn't, but I didn't correct her. "I have an idea," I said. "There's a small park about half a mile from here. It has a lot of trees, and you can let the boys run and play without fear of being seen."

She bit her lip. "I don't know…"

"Take my car so even if Ken drives by, he won't see yours." I extended the keys toward her. Yes, I was willing to let her take my beloved car just so I could have a few hours of peace and quiet.

She set the butterfly carefully on the coffee table, her gaze caressing it. I usually feel the same way about crystal. Looking at the rainbows, touching the smooth edges…very soothing. But not this time. I didn't want it in my house. I would be thrilled to turn it over to Trent and let his lab do whatever they wanted with it. In the meantime…

"And take the butterfly with you. Focus on the rainbows in the crystal and try not to think about…other things."

Tina left with my keys, the butterfly, and a promise to return in a couple of hours. I wasn't sure if that was a promise or a threat.

The ensuing silence throbbed against my eardrums. Or maybe my eardrums still throbbed from all the noise.

Henry recovered immediately and strolled toward the kitchen, turning his head to be sure I was following.

"I know you think I'm crazy to let them take my car." I fell into step behind him. He is, after all, King Henry, and his wishes must be obeyed. Besides, I desperately needed a Coke fix and my Cokes live in the same room where his food lives.

"It's not like one more scratch or ding on my car is going to make a difference. Brandon's going to take care of all that when he gets a new job somewhere away from his creepy father." We entered the kitchen and Henry went straight to his bowl. I took the bag of cat food out of the pantry. "If Grady Mathis goes to prison, maybe Brandon will inherit the family shop. I don't know what happens to property when somebody goes to prison."

Henry didn't know either and didn't care. He looked into his empty bowl then up at me. I filled his bowl in accordance with his wishes.

Then it was my turn. I opened the refrigerator door and reached inside the red cardboard carton that held my beverage of choice.

It was empty.

That was not possible.

I yanked it out and peered inside.

Nothing.

I ripped it apart.

No Cokes. Not one.

And I didn't have a car to go get any.

Henry crunched his food, completely unconcerned about my disaster.

213

At least I had the bag of chocolate I'd brought home with me.

Except I didn't. I'd been talking on the phone to Trent and had forgotten to bring my bag in from the car. The bag with whatever might be left in it currently resided in my car at the park. That sort of verified Trent's nags about my inability to multi-task while I'm on the phone. Not that I would ever admit it to him.

But all was not lost. I still had the box of Godiva chocolates Trent had given me.

I opened the pantry door and reached up.

My hand encountered only empty space. I must have shoved them farther to the back than I realized.

I pulled over a kitchen chair and stood on it.

The shelf was empty.

The Hyper Horde had eaten my Godiva chocolates! When I told Tina they could eat whatever they could find, I hadn't thought they'd find those chocolates.

I stepped down from the chair and Henry came over to rub against my leg as if trying to comfort me in my hour of sorrow.

"Heads are going to roll over this."

He purred and rubbed the other leg. Either he was very sympathetic or he was hoping to get catnip.

I gave him catnip. One of us should have a fix.

While Henry indulged himself, I searched for Brandon's business card. I finally found it in the living room, missing a corner and smeared with magic markers. I hoped Drake had no plans to become an artist.

I called the number on the front and the number on the back. Got the same recording on both with Grady's voice saying I'd reached Mathis Paint and Body Shop. I hung up without leaving a message. Poor Brandon didn't even have his own cell phone.

Henry strolled in from the kitchen, his steps slow and his eyes slightly crossed. He enjoyed his catnip.

"I'm going upstairs to take a nap," I said. "I need to be rested so I can stay up late with Trent. He invited you to come along, but I told him you'd be fine here. I know you don't like riding in cars. No, I didn't tell him about your phobia. That's between you and me."

Henry went to the front door and I let him out then went upstairs to enjoy a long, solitary shower before collapsing in bed.

∂∾∽

A loud ringing woke me. I sat up, completely disoriented. My bedroom window showed a dim light. The sun was coming up! I was late for work!

The noise came again.

It wasn't the alarm clock.

Six thirty.

The sun was setting, not rising. I'd slept almost three hours.

The doorbell pealed a third time, and I came completely awake. Probably Tina and the Hyper Horde returning from the park. I'd wasted my quiet time sleeping.

Damn!

I went downstairs and peered through the peephole. I wasn't taking any chances. Tina had no

215

reason to knock since she had my keys, including a key to my house, and besides, Grady was still out there.

Brandon, alive and unharmed, stood on my front porch wearing his usual jeans and denim work shirt.

With a huge rush of relief, I opened the door. "Well, hello! It's so good to see you! I was worried when you didn't come in for lunch today."

"I'm fine. I was just getting my new place cleaned up."

A few dark spots on his usually immaculate jeans and shirt verified that he'd been working. "You found a place? That's wonderful! Come in and tell me all about it!"

"How about I take you there and show you?"

I hesitated. Being at home hadn't been pleasant lately, but I didn't really feel up to oohing and aahing over an apartment. "I don't know. I have company. They went to the park, but they'll be back any time."

"It's not far, only about ten minutes from here."

"Oh. I thought you were going to find something as far away from your dad as you could get."

He shrugged. "You'll understand when you see the place."

Listen to Tina's kids or go look at Brandon's apartment? Trent wouldn't be here for at least another hour. If I spent half an hour praising Brandon's apartment, that would be half an hour I wouldn't have to spend with the Hyper Horde, leaving only half an hour before Trent arrived on his white charger—well, in his black sedan—to rescue me. It would also give me a chance to talk to

Brandon and convince him to give the cops permission to search his house and place of business.

That tilted the decision in Brandon's favor. Trent would be impressed if I got that permission, and maybe then they'd be able to find Grady and arrest him.

"I'd love to see your new apartment. I loaned my car to a friend. Can I ride with you?"

He looked surprised. "You loaned your car to someone?"

"It's a long story."

"I'd like to hear your story."

I didn't want to talk about Tina's situation. "After we look at your new place."

He smiled. "I'd love for you to ride with me."

I grabbed my purse and followed him down the sidewalk to his car, the same car he'd driven the day he bumped into me, the day that began our friendship and resulted in me persuading him to leave his abusive father. That was a good thing.

However, a shiver ran down my spine as I reflected that it was also the day that resulted in my meeting Grady Mathis.

But Trent and Fred were on Grady's trail. I'd get Brandon's permission to search, and soon Grady would be behind bars. "Getting your own place is a huge step! I'm so proud of you. What did your dad say when you told him?"

Brandon opened the car door for me and I slid in.

"I haven't told him," he said.

That didn't surprise me. Brandon had good reason to fear his father. "That's okay. Maybe you can just disappear and never have to confront him."

He got in the other side and started the engine.

"Have you talked to your dad at all since his outburst at my place yesterday?"

Brandon steered the car onto the street and shook his head, his lips compressed.

"The police are looking for him, you know."

He nodded.

"They'd like for you to agree to let them search the house and the shop."

"Can we talk about something else? This is a pretty big deal for me, and I don't want to ruin it by talking about that man right now."

"Of course we can talk about something else. Tell me about your new place."

જ≈

Ten minutes later we pulled into the driveway of an older house. The place wasn't charming old with lots of personality like the houses in my neighborhood. It was boring old. These houses were probably built in the '50s or '60s. Small slab homes with no basements. That's almost unheard of in Kansas City. Everybody has to have a basement so they can worry about cracks and leaks.

"What do you think?" he asked.

"It's, uh, lovely. Are you renting a room or is there an apartment in back?"

He smiled proudly. "I have the whole house."

218

"Well. Okay. This is, um, very nice." Another blatant lie so ridiculous no one could possibly believe it.

He opened his car door then came around and opened mine. "Come see inside. I've spent all day getting it ready."

I did not want to see inside, but it was obviously important to him. This was no time for me to be snobbish. I planted my feet on the cracked driveway and stood. "I can't wait."

We walked to the front door and he produced a key. "We can replace this," he said, indicating the faded hollow core door with water damage on the bottom.

"Sure," I said. "Easy to replace a door."

"I think one of those pretty ones with glass."

"Of course." A heavy oak door with beveled glass insets would be a lovely compliment to the warped beige siding.

I stepped onto the gold shag carpet of the living room. Irrationally the sound of the door closing behind me was disturbing. Actually, the whole place was disturbing. A sagging couch sat in front of a new flat screen TV. On one side of the sofa a floor lamp had age-yellowed plastic wrap around the shade.

It was all clean and tidy. I couldn't spot a sign of dust. Nevertheless, the place smelled like cigarette smoke and mold.

I turned to Brandon who smiled tentatively. "Did this place come furnished?" *Please tell me you didn't go out and buy this horrible stuff!*

219

"Yes. It's not much to look at now but I have lots of plans to make it nicer."

"Great." I braced myself to see the rest of the house.

"Do you like it?"

"Um, sure." All that practice lying to traffic cops was paying off.

He proudly showed me the kitchen with contact paper over pressed wood cabinets, the bathroom with rust stains in the tub, and two bedrooms with sagging mattresses. He paused at the door of the larger bedroom.

"This is the master."

I surveyed the room with its matched set of 1950s furniture, all surfaces clean, and an obviously new spread on the bed.

"It's very nice," I said.

"So you like it?"

I did not. "I do."

He beamed down at me. I tried to return his smile. The room was ugly and the house was ugly, but he looked happy. I suspected Brandon didn't have much happiness in his life.

I lifted my wrist and pointed at my watch. "Gosh, how did it get to be so late? I'd better get home. My company should be back by now."

He laughed softly. "Don't worry about your company."

He probably meant to be reassuring, but his comment irritated me. Much as I would have liked to completely forget about my company, that would have been rude.

I went down the hallway to the lovely living room.

Brandon followed close behind me. "So you really like it?" he asked again. "You're not just saying that?"

"You've done a great job." I looked at my watch again.

He stepped closer, lifted my hair off my neck and pressed his lips to my neck.

Holy crap!

I jerked away and whirled to face him.

He blinked rapidly, a dazed expression on his face.

I tried to assure myself he had not gone bat crap crazy, that he'd just been carried away with showing me his new home, sharing his pride in making the escape from his father.

"Lindsay, what's wrong?" He reached for my hands.

I tucked them behind my back and took another step away from him. "What's wrong?" That was a very good question. I wasn't sure what the answer was. Maybe I was overreacting. I've been accused of that before. But suddenly I was frantic to be out of that house and away from Brandon. The alternative, spending time with Tina's horde, seemed like a visit to a butterfly garden compared to this creepy place. "Uhhh...my visitors. It's very rude for me not to be there with them. Love the house, I'm proud of you for making the break, and I need to go now."

He smiled his sweet, innocent smile and I drew in a deep breath of relief. Everything was fine. Tour of the tawdry house was over and I'd soon be home with Henry and the Hyper Horde.

But Brandon moved closer, invading my space, making me extremely uncomfortable. I stepped backward again…and ran into the wall.

He shook his head and continued to smile. "You're so darned cute, Lindsay." He put a hand on my cheek and leaned toward me as if to kiss me.

That did it. I was officially freaked out. I shoved against his chest. "Brandon, stop that! Take me home, now!"

His smile disappeared and his whole face changed so drastically I would not have recognized him if I hadn't seen it happen. His mouth turned down, his cheeks reddened and his eyes bulged. "This is your home."

I blinked, trying to clear my vision and make sense of what was going on.

As quickly as the monster had overtaken Brandon's face, it disappeared and the sunny smile and puppy dog eyes were back. I felt as if I'd lost touch with reality, was having a bad nightmare where familiar people morphed into demons and back into human beings at random.

"We're going to be so happy here." He reached into his pocket then extended a hand toward me. "I got this back for you."

I cringed away from him as my gaze dropped to the object in his hand.

The damned butterfly. The butterfly Grady had left on my porch. The butterfly I'd given to Tina. "Where did you get that?"

"That woman stole it from you, but I took it away from her."

The walls of the living room, the sagging sofa, and the coffee table with chipped veneer all blurred. Only Brandon and the crystal butterfly in his hand were clear and vivid, almost glowing in intensity.

"*That woman?*" Each word stuck on my tongue as I pushed it out.

"The one that took your car. I followed her to the park."

"You followed her?"

He shrugged and looked pleased with himself. "I followed the tracker I put on your car when you brought it into the shop. I wanted to be able to find you if you needed my help, and you did. When I saw that woman sitting in your car, I dragged her out. I thought she stole it, but she said you loaned it to her."

"I did." My voice was barely a whisper and I wasn't sure if he heard. It probably didn't matter anyway.

"She had your butterfly in her hand. She was trying to steal it. I got it away from her."

Suddenly the spots on his clothing took on a new significance. They were small and dark and maybe they weren't spots of dirt or grease. "What did you do to Tina?"

"I punished her for stealing from you. Taking our butterfly was even worse than that woman with red hair who came to your house and yelled at you." He smiled and moved closer and I tried to back inside the wall.

"You…" I gulped, licked my lips and tried again to speak. "You punished Tina like you punished the woman with red hair?" I thought of Fred's theory that Grady had been trying to help me by killing people who annoyed me.

"Nobody's ever going to hurt you again."

I was surely hallucinating. Kind, gentle Brandon could not be saying what I thought he was saying, that he'd killed Ginger and Tina. Appearances can certainly be deceiving. I'd been frightened of Bob when I first met him, and he'd been a kind, gentle person. Brandon had given the appearance of a teddy bear. I upgraded that image to a grizzly bear with rabies.

"What about Tina's kids?"

He shook his head. "Kids? I didn't see any kids."

I could only hope the kids hadn't seen their mother being murdered.

I turned and ran for the front door. I seemed to be moving in slow motion, each step like walking through waist high sand. After an eternity I made it, grabbed the door knob and twisted.

It refused to turn.

He'd locked it.

My stomach squeezed into a hard, painful knot.

Yeah, nobody was ever going to hurt me again— nobody except him.

He grabbed my shoulder from behind.

I twisted away and darted to the door on the side of the room. Mercifully the knob turned. I yanked it open.

"No!" Brandon shouted.

Garage. No light, but I could see the outlines of objects, tools and car pieces. Surely I could find a weapon. I sprinted inside.

I stumbled and put my hand out to break my fall. My purse slid off my shoulder and my fingers touched something squishy.

The overhead light flashed on and I saw that my hand rested on a bloody, battered mass that used to be Grady Mathis' head.

Holy crap.

Chapter Sixteen

"I'm so sorry. I didn't want you to see the mess." Brandon stood in the doorway to the garage. "I'll clean it up."

The walls around me closed in then moved back out. Brandon loomed ten feet high then shrank to normal size. The whole scene was a surreal nightmare. I had just stumbled over a dead body, the body of a man I'd served chocolate to only a few days ago, a man who'd yelled at me and smashed my cell phone. Brandon's father. His father was dead and Brandon was concerned with the mess? I struggled to my feet. "You...did this?"

He beamed. "He hurt you. I couldn't let him get away with that. Nobody hurts the woman I love."

Oh, great. Now I could feel responsible for the murders of Tina, Ginger and Grady.

I could maybe live with the blame for Grady's death, but not the others.

Brandon extended his hand to me. The last thing in the world I wanted to do was touch that man.

I hesitated and realized that wasn't quite true. The last thing in the world I wanted to do was get murdered by that man.

I picked up my purse by one side of the strap. The rest was covered in bits of Grady's head. I hadn't liked that head when it was all one piece and attached to his body. I really didn't like carrying parts of it with me, but my cell phone was in that purse. I needed to call Trent or Fred.

What was it I'd said when Paula remarked that Fred and Trent had saved my neck a couple of times?

I would have been fine even if they hadn't showed up.

It's easy to be cocky when there's no madman around.

I accepted Brandon's hand, swallowed my gag reflex and stepped over his father's body to join him in the house he'd prepared for us.

He wrapped an arm around my waist. "If you'll cook dinner, I'll do the dishes."

Oh, sure, let's just forget about the corpse in the garage and have a nice dinner.

"Actually, I've been cooking all day. I'd really like to go out to eat." Get him in a public place and I could get away or at least make a phone call.

Brandon tapped the end of my nose with his finger and smiled some more. I once thought he had a charming smile. Who knew there was such a thin line between charming and psycho?

"We can order pizza," he said. "I know you like pizza because I've seen lots of deliveries to your house. I want you all to myself for our first night in our new home."

I wasn't sure which creeped me out more—the fact that he wanted me all to himself or the fact that he'd been watching me for so long he knew I ate a lot of pizza. Just how long had he been watching me?

"Remember when you ran into my car?" I asked.

227

"Of course."

"That wasn't an accident, was it?"

"Don't you worry about your car. I'll fix it good as new."

"I mean, you did it on purpose. To..." I swallowed. "To get my attention."

He smiled that boyish smile again. "You were always so busy in the restaurant, you never had time to talk. But I knew you noticed me. I could tell by the way you looked at me. We just needed an excuse to get to know each other better." He pulled me close to his side as we walked back to the living room. If only I'd had Fred teach me Karate or whatever that stuff was that he did.

Brandon put the damned butterfly on the coffee table and pulled me onto the sofa beside him. I dropped my purse over the side, hiding it from him but keeping it close, then tried to calm my racing mind and heart and focus on what I needed to do. He loved me. With any sort of luck, that meant he wasn't planning to kill me. All I had to do was lead him on until I could escape.

He wrapped both arms around me and again leaned in for a kiss.

I tilted my head backward and shoved him away. His face darkened and swelled. The outraged ogre took over again.

"Not until we're married!" I blurted. And that day was never going to come.

"You kissed that cop on your front porch and you hugged that homeless man!" His features contorted even more.

The sound of wind chimes filled the room. How sweet. Trent had set the new phone's ring tone to the one I had on my old phone.

Brandon shot up from the sofa and looked around. "What's that noise?"

My phone was drawing attention to itself. Not good. "One of your neighbors must have wind chimes. Come back and sit here beside me." I patted the sofa.

"It's your purse." He picked it up. "What's this all over it?"

Bits and pieces of your father's head.

"Uh...I dropped it in something."

Disgust spread over his face. Ironic since he was the one who'd caused the mess in the first place.

My purse continued to chime.

He dumped the contents on the coffee table. A pen, a lipstick, my checkbook, my wallet, a candy bar, and my cell phone. He snatched up the phone and answered. "Who is this?" He glowered at me as he listened to the response. "Well, Detective Adam Trent, Lindsay doesn't want to talk to you. Don't call her again." He threw the phone across the room. My heart sank as my chance to call Trent or Fred shattered against the wall. The Mathis men were hard on cell phones.

He threw the gory purse on the coffee table then, without warning, drew back his fist and slammed it into my face, rocking my head backward. For an instant I didn't believe that sweet, gentle Brandon had punched me. Anger and fear shot through me followed by intense pain and the taste of blood. So much for thinking he wouldn't hurt me because he loved me.

He stood over me, leaning down, shouting at me, his demented face only inches from mine, his breath hot on my cheeks. "I've always been faithful to you! How can you say you love me when you've been with another man?"

I was one hundred percent certain I'd never said I loved him but I didn't argue the point. I sat straighter and glared at him. "Men don't hit women," I said quietly, "especially women they claim to love."

Again his fist slammed into my face, this time on the other side. "You made me do it! You've been cheating on me!"

Reason and retaliation hadn't worked so well. I wiped the blood from my lips and tried to figure out the right response to his accusations. What would make Mr. Hyde revert to Dr. Jekyll before I ran out of cheeks to turn? Much as I hated the thought of pacifying someone who'd just punched me, I had neither Karate skills nor gun so I had to do it.

"I…" *I* what? I was not going to tell someone who'd just hit me that I loved him. "I didn't know."

He stood straighter. The crazy eyes bulged a little less. "You didn't know what?"

"I didn't know how you felt." I swallowed and tasted my own blood. That was not a good thing. I forced myself to say whatever it took to keep the rest of that blood in my veins where it belonged. "I didn't know you loved me."

"I brought you gifts. I wrote poems for you. I got rid of the people you didn't like. You put the butterfly with your cookies to let me know you love me too."

He was calmer. No less crazy, but calmer.

"I just couldn't believe you really…" I swallowed again. My tongue touched a molar on the left side. It wiggled. I hate going to the dentist. I wanted to punch him and loosen a bunch of his teeth. Brandon's teeth, not the dentist's. But I wasn't big enough or strong enough. I had to force myself to continue sucking up to him.

"I couldn't believe you really loved me. But now that I know you do…" *Now that I know you do*…what? *I'll run when I see you instead of going to an empty house with you? I'll put the closed sign on Death by Chocolate when I see you coming? I'll bring a chain saw to our next meeting?* Probably not what he wanted to hear. "I'll be a better woman."

The smile returned to his face and he sat down beside me again. "I've looked for you all my life. You've made me a better man. I was nobody until I found you."

Terrific. He found me and changed from nobody to a crazed murderer. What a wonderful influence to have on a person. My mother would be so proud.

"You mentioned a homeless man." I didn't want to wake the beast again, but I needed to know just how much mayhem had been committed in my name. "Did you punish the homeless man in the alley behind Death by Chocolate?"

"He tried to force himself on you. I saw him put his arms around you."

Actually, I'd hugged Bob, but this was not the time to correct Brandon's misconception.

"Uh, yeah, thank you for protecting me." *If you're listening, Bob, I'm sorry! I didn't mean it! I'm lying to survive!*

"I let you down with your ex-husband. He's stronger than he looks. He fought back and blacked my eye."

Rick had blacked Brandon's eye? How dumb could I have been? Rick told me he fought with his attacker, hurt the man, but I hadn't believed him. The black eye must have been a lucky punch. Rick was not strong, but he was lucky.

I forced myself to touch the fading bruise around Brandon's eye. "Rick is a very bad man." I wasn't lying that time.

Brandon grabbed my wrist and brought my palm to his lips. I tried not to shudder.

"I'll take care of him when he gets out of the hospital," he said.

I bared my teeth in an attempt at a smile. "Great. Thank you."

"As soon as I get rid of your ex-husband and that sleazy cop who called you and was pawing all over you on your front porch, we can get married and be happy."

A slow, dark anger rose from my clenched stomach and spread through my chest replacing the fear. Brandon had just signed his own death warrant. How dare he talk that way about the man I lo—cared about! If Trent didn't kill him, I would.

"You know what would make me very happy right now?" I asked.

He laid a hand on my cheek. I tried not to flinch from revulsion and pain. "Whatever it is, I'll do it for you, sweetheart."

"I'd really like a Coke, a nice cold Coke. You know how I love Coke."

He grinned. "I sure do know how much you love Coke. I know everything about my girl."

Not quite everything. Not what happened when somebody insulted my cat, my friends, my chocolate chip cookies, or my boyfriend. "Let's go get a Coke."

"We don't have to go anywhere. I've got a fresh case of Cokes in the refrigerator."

Oh, yay.

"Would you get me one, please?" I bared my teeth again.

If I could get him in the kitchen, I could escape through the garage. Never mind that I'd have to step over Grady's body again. I would do whatever it took to get away.

He stood and I tensed, ready to run as soon as he got to the kitchen and stuck his head in the refrigerator.

But he held out his hand. "Come with me. I want you by my side every minute for at least the next fifty years."

I stretched the teeth-baring gesture to show my molars, including the one that wiggled suspiciously. "Me too."

I rose and followed him into the kitchen. Now I knew how Tina and Paula had felt—the helplessness and fear, the attempts to placate someone they despised to avoid further pain. I was proud that I'd helped put Paula's ex behind bars. It was too late for Tina, but when I got away from Brandon, I would see that Ken paid for the torture he'd inflicted on her.

While my captor ripped into the carton of Cokes in the refrigerator, I looked around the room more closely than I had on the initial tour. The harvest gold countertop held a set of plastic canisters, a can opener, a couple of trivets, a coffee maker and other objects that indicated someone lived there. Unfortunately, I did not see a knife block. I'd been hoping to find a nice sharp filet knife.

I started to open a drawer then hesitated. "Okay if I look in here?" I cannot find the words to describe how badly it galled me to ask for permission.

"Of course, sweetheart. This is your home too."

I slid open a drawer. Silverware but no knives. I opened another one. Spatulas, mixing spoons, potato masher, and a metal meat tenderizer. I wrapped my hand around the cold handle of the tenderizer and lifted it out. Drawing my arm back, I spun around toward Brandon and brought the tenderizer in an arc aimed for his head.

He grabbed my wrist. "You bitch!"

Damnation! I'd awakened the fiend again. He twisted my arm until I dropped the tenderizer and continued twisting until he forced me to the floor.

"See what you made me do? Clean that up!"

He released my arm and I realized I was sitting in a puddle of something cold and wet. A red can lay

on its side, spilling brown liquid on the floor. The
Coke Brandon had opened for me.

Strictly speaking, I had made him drop the Coke
when I tried to kill him. But if he hadn't forced me to
stay in this place, I wouldn't have tried to kill him.
Ultimately it was his fault the Coke was spilled. And
now I had another reason to hate him. Wasted Coke.

"All I ever did was love you!" He strode back
and forth across the floor, tearing at his hair. "Why
do you treat me like this? I got rid of Mother for you
and you didn't appreciate it!"

I got rid of Mother? My heart froze and dropped
to the floor. He'd killed my mother? She drives me
crazy and I complain about her, but she's my mother!
"Why would you hurt my mother?"

He stopped, blinked a couple of times, then
frowned. "Your mother? I don't know your mother."

I drew in a deep breath, marginally relieved,
though this guy was so out of it, I still wasn't certain.
"You said you got rid of Mother."

He blinked again then smiled. "Not your mother,
sweetheart. My mother. She didn't take care of me.
You're going to be a great mother. You'll never let
anybody hurt our children."

Our children? I grabbed his leg and brought him
tumbling down beside me. He scrambled around and
pinned me to the floor, looming over me. "You
worthless tramp! You're a pig who wallows in the
mud with the other pigs! You kissed that man on
your porch in front of me! He called you in our
home!" He turned loose of my arms, grabbed my

head and pounded it against the floor. "I'm going to kill you!"

I believed him.

Rage brighter and hotter than an oil well fire in west Texas burst over me at the thought that this man could end my life, make Henry an orphan with nobody to feed him or give him catnip, keep me from Zach's high school graduation, take me away from Trent before I got up the courage to tell him how I felt about him. I would do whatever it took to get away from this monster. I would survive, give Henry some extra catnip, make more moldy cookies for Zach, and tell Trent I loved him.

My hands shot to his arms, but I forced myself to be calm, to think rather than react. Instead of trying to pull them away, I stroked his arms. He stopped banging my head. When this was over, I was going to have to spend a week with my chiropractor.

If I lived through this.

I looked into Brandon's crazy eyes and said the first words that came to my mind. "I thought you were cheating on me like Rick used to. I was trying to get revenge."

He opened his mouth then closed it and frowned. Slowly Psycho Brandon receded. "I'd never cheat on you. I love you."

"I know that now. I'm so sorry I didn't trust you. It'll never happen again."

He smiled but made no move to get off me.

"I'd really like a cold Coke and a hot pizza to, you know, celebrate our…" *Puke.* "Love."

He rose, opened the refrigerator door and took out another Coke, popped the top and handed the can to me. "Straight up, no ice, just the way you like it."

"Thank you." I took a drink, letting the cold bubbles flow over my tongue and down my throat. It cooled my tongue and soothed my throat but did nothing to dampen the anger boiling inside me.

My feet were sticky from the spilled Coke, but I didn't want to bring that up. If he could ignore it, so could I. "This house, somebody lives here. You didn't rent it, did you?"

"Oh, no, we own it." He lifted the receiver from the wall phone. "What's the number for pizza delivery?"

I told him the number and he punched it in.

"We own this house? Is this where you and your father live? Lived?"

"I'd like a large double pepperoni pizza." He gave the address then hung up and turned to me with a proud smile on his face. "The house is ours now. He killed Mother and now he's dead too so we own it."

His father killed his mother? Hadn't he just said he'd killed her? No, he said he got rid of her. So his father killed her and he got rid of the body? Two generations of murderers. What a terrific heritage for those children Brandon was planning.

I sat down at the kitchen table. The chairs were wooden. I felt much better about sitting on them than on the soft sofa that oozed up around me. "Did you just say your father killed your mother?"

He opened a can of Coke for himself and joined me at the table. His expression was grim but not crazy grim. How many personalities did this guy have?

"He cheated on her, hit her, bullied her, hurt her and made her cry."

"And then he killed her? Was it an accident?"

He sat rigidly still for a long moment. I tensed, wondering if my questions had set him off again, if I'd survive the next attack. I squared my jaw. I would survive the next attack. And the next and the next. I would get out of this alive though I might have to get dentures afterward.

He looked over my head, staring at the wall. Or maybe he was just gazing into his own sick mind. "She didn't stop him from hitting me. She didn't love me. Daddy said it was all her fault because she got pregnant with me. He said he never wanted to be married. So I gave her lots of her pills. She died but he kept hitting me anyway." His gaze returned to mine. "It was his fault she had to die. And now he's dead. He's never going to hurt you or our children."

Those children again! Before this was over, I'd make sure he'd never be able to have children. Or I'd die and at least he and I wouldn't have children together. "I think you're probably right about your father never hurting anybody again." I took another drink of Coke, a long one.

He laid his hand over mine on the table and gazed at me with those puppy dog eyes. I might never be able to have a dog after making that association.

I shot to my feet, yanking my hand away. The front door and garage were out as escape routes. But there had to be other possibilities. "I need to go to the bathroom. That Coke, it just goes right through me."

"Does my baby have a tiny bladder?"

"About the size of a walnut. Gotta go."

He led me down the hall past the bedrooms to a bathroom at the end. "I cleared a space under the sink for you to put your shampoo and all that stuff women have."

"You're so thoughtful." I walked into the tiny room. No window to crawl out. Damn. I closed the door behind me, relieved he didn't follow me in, but there was no lock on the door to keep him out.

A tub with a shower. Small sink with a soap dish holding a new bar of soap and a glass with an old toothbrush and a new one. I assumed the new one was for me. I wiggled the loose tooth again. If he hit me a few more times, I wouldn't need that new toothbrush.

I looked under the sink. Men's cologne. Shampoo. Plastic hair dryer. Nothing even remotely resembling a weapon.

"Lindsay? Are you okay?"

"Nervous bladder. First time in a new place. Just need a few minutes."

He chuckled. "But not the last time!"

I opened the medicine cabinet. Pay dirt! Drugs. If it had worked for Brandon, it could work for me.

I reached over and flushed the toilet to cover the noise of the pills rattling when I took out the brown bottles to look at the labels. I had no idea what they were but found one that said, *Do not drive or operate machinery while taking this drug. May cause drowsiness.*

The prescription was five years old. Did drugs lose their potency with age?

There were fifteen or twenty small white capsules in that bottle. I didn't take time to count. I put them all in my pocket, opened the door and smiled at Brandon. That time my smile was genuine. I planned to give a whole new meaning to Death by Chocolate.

Chapter Seventeen

"I have a great idea," I said. "Let's have some hot chocolate."

He frowned and I tensed, one hand on the bathroom door, ready to jump back inside and slam the door if the demon reappeared.

"I don't have any hot chocolate mix," he said.

I breathed again and waved a hand dismissively. "We don't need that. Did you forget I'm a chocolatier? I never use a mix." That wasn't even close to true, but it was no bigger lie than telling him I'd be a better woman because of him.

I scooted past, dodging his attempts to touch me. The man had grown at least four extra hands since we'd entered that house.

"I need sugar, cocoa and milk," I called over my shoulder as I raced down the hall toward the kitchen.

A brown puddle stained the floor. I'd forgotten about the spilled Coke. I grabbed some paper towels and began cleaning as fast as I could. I didn't want the mess to remind Brandon of my attempt to smash his head. It might make him go nuts again. Worse, it might make him so cautious I wouldn't be able to poison him.

"Let me help." He squatted on the floor beside me.

"Not necessary." I stood. "All done. Now for the hot chocolate." I began yanking open cabinet doors. He came up behind me and I tried to open a door into his face, but he ducked. I continued opening and closing doors and pretended it didn't happen.

Suddenly he wrapped his arms around me from behind. Crap. He didn't believe the door incident was an accident and was going to punch me again.

He lowered his head to my neck and nuzzled. If I'd had a choice, I'd probably have chosen the punch. "My silly darling," he murmured. "We have lots of time for hot chocolate this winter. I have plenty of Cokes for now."

I touched my pocket with its reassuring small bulges and forced myself to endure the nuzzling. "No, I need hot chocolate. Now. Surely you know I'm addicted to chocolate. I could go into withdrawal if I don't get some chocolate soon."

He laughed, his breath hot and humid on my neck.

I shivered and, inspired, continued the involuntary movement by twitching first one arm then the other. "See? The DTs are already starting."

He stepped back and gave a fond sigh. "Whatever my baby wants. I've got milk." He opened the refrigerator door to show me a carton of skim milk. I preferred regular, but it wasn't as if I expected this hot chocolate to taste good.

"Great. I assume you have sugar in one of those canisters. Now all we need is cocoa."

He looked blank.

Damn. How could he think to buy Cokes but not cocoa when I specialized in chocolate? What kind of stalker was he anyway?

"Sometimes Mama used to make hot chocolate for me after Daddy hit me." His voice was soft, his expression distant as if he was looking into the past. He walked slowly to the pantry and opened the door. I'd already looked in there. Canned peas, coffee, boxes of macaroni and cheese. Nothing useful.

He reached far in the back of a high shelf and emerged with a familiar and beloved maroon colored container. My spirits soared. The poisoning event was on.

He extended the box to me tentatively. "It's old. It may be spoiled."

I accepted the cocoa with a smile. "Cocoa doesn't spoil." I didn't know that for a fact as I'd always used my cocoa long before it had a chance to reach possible spoilage date. "Why, they've found cocoa in Aztec tombs that made quite excellent hot chocolate."

"Really?"

I had no idea, but it sounded plausible. "Of course! Now you just go relax in the living room and watch TV while I make us some hot cocoa."

He sat down at the table. "I want to be with you. I can't believe you're finally mine."

"Neither can I. Where are the saucepans?"

He smiled and pointed to one of the lower cabinet doors. "In there."

I opened the door. A jumble of pots and pans, all old and light weight. No iron skillet. Damn. I'd hoped to find one in case the pills didn't work. Or in addition to the pills.

I selected a saucepan and turned around. "Found it!"

I took a spoon from the silverware drawer, mixed cocoa and sugar with a small amount of water and set it on the stove.

"I love watching you cook," Brandon said.

I kept stirring. "Where are the cups?"

"I'll get them."

I did not want him near me where he could watch too closely. I turned and showed my teeth. "Oh, no, I want you to just sit there and let me do this for you."

He beamed. "All right, sweetheart. The cups are in the cabinet over the coffee maker."

"Thank you." I batted my eyes and opened the cabinet door. Three of the white mugs had messages on them. *I (heart) chocolate. Life is short; eat chocolate first. Lindsay's mug.*

Holy crap. Suddenly Grady's flirtation with me made more sense. He must have known about his son's obsession. Possibly he had tried to get me to hook up with him in an effort to torment his already-abused son. I felt a little sorry for Brandon. Not sorry enough to let him live, however.

I took down my mug and the *I (heart) chocolate* one.

While I mixed the drugs with the cocoa, I needed to divert his attention from my cooking, find something he was obsessed with besides me.

"What do you think about those Royals?" All men were obsessed with football.

"You mean the baseball team?"

I measured two cups of milk into the saucepan using the heart mug so it would have a little milk in the bottom. "Whatever. Think they'll make it to the Superbowl?"

He laughed. "My silly lady. The Superbowl is football. You don't have to pretend to be interested in that stuff. I know you don't watch sports."

I shuddered, imagining him outside my window, watching me watching *Castle, Bones, Person of Interest* and *Big Bang Theory* but no ball games.

"I thought you might be interested. You look like maybe you played football in high school." I stirred the hot chocolate with one hand while the other hand slipped some of the capsules out of my pocket. I pressed against the white coating with my thumbnail, trying to split it.

"I didn't like high school." He sounded irritated. Damn. What could I talk about that wouldn't upset him?

"How many children do you think we should have?" Blasted capsule was tougher than it looked. I have no trouble piercing the plastic seal on a can of cocoa with that thumbnail. I finally made a slit and dropped the whole thing into the quarter inch of milk in the bottom of the cup. The capsules were made to dissolve in someone's stomach. With any luck, they'd dissolve in the milk.

"I think two, a boy and a girl." He sounded happy. I'd found the key. Feed his delusions. "But if you want three, we can talk about it."

Tina had three. What would those boys do without their mother? My anger gave extra strength to my thumbnail. I burst open a capsule and dumped the contents into the cup then put the shell back in my pocket. Capsules weren't so strong when I was appropriately angry. I added two more then a little extra cocoa and sugar to hide whatever taste the drugs might have.

The beverage began to steam. "Almost done." My voice rose to a falsetto. "I hope you like it. I'll make it for our son and daughter one day."

"You know I'll love it."

I dumped another couple of capsules into the heart cup then poured in the steaming chocolate and stirred Brandon's special blend very fast. "You know what would make this really good? Putting it in a blender until it's all foamy." *And the pills are completely dissolved.*

"We don't have a blender, but I'll get you one tomorrow."

I'd have to settle for extra stirring. I set both cups on the table, the doctored brew in front of Brandon, then sat down and sipped from my cup.

Brandon frowned.

I froze in mid-sip. What had I done now?

"That's my cup."

Damn! "It has my name on it."

"I always drink out of that cup."

"I've already drunk out of it."

246

He smiled. "I don't mind drinking after you."

I tried to imitate a puppy begging for a treat. "Please? I want to drink out of the cup you drank from yesterday." I held the cup under discussion between both hands and tilted my head to one side. I wasn't sure if I was doing it right since I don't have a dog. I only have a cat who looks at me threateningly when he wants a treat. I didn't think a threatening look was likely to get me anywhere with Brandon.

He melted. "If that's what my baby wants, that's what she'll get."

"Bottoms up!"

I lifted my cup to my lips and watched Brandon take a drink. He grimaced. Guess the taste of drugs trumped the taste of chocolate.

"What do you think?" I asked. "Do you like my cocoa?"

"It tastes—"

"Yummy! I know!"

I drank some more.

He didn't.

"Don't you like the chocolate I made for you?"

"It's not as good as the desserts you make at your restaurant."

"It's the skim milk. I always use whole milk or half and half at the restaurant."

"It tastes...funny."

I sniffed and wiped my eyes then let out a loud wail. "You don't like my cocoa! I can't bear it!" I laid my head on the table and made sobbing noises.

"I do like it! See, I'm drinking it!"

I lifted my head. "I'm so glad. I couldn't stand it if you didn't like my cooking. I live to cook for you. I'll be your own personal chocolatier from now on. You'll see. We're going to be so happy. Just you and me and Brandon Jr. and little Lindsay." I hoped the drug took effect rapidly. I wasn't sure how many more absurdities I could spin.

He drained his cup then looked inside. "You didn't get all the sugar stirred up. No wonder it tasted funny."

I snatched the mug away from him. "How could I be so careless?" *So careless not to get all the pills dissolved.* I hoped he'd swallowed enough to take him down. "Here, have some of mine." I offered him my cup.

He took it and sipped then smiled. "I love putting my lips where yours have been."

Yuck. "Drink up and let's go to the living room and hold hands until the pizza gets here."

"I'd like that."

He followed me to the living room where my gory purse rested on the coffee table on top of my wallet and lipstick. I averted my gaze and steeled myself to sit on the musty sofa and hold his hand for—how long? Ten minutes? Fifteen? I could do anything for that long. I once held a frog for five minutes. Of course, I was in the third grade and Ronnie Duncan dared me at recess.

I sat on the sofa.

He sat beside me and took my hand.

Frog. I'd held the frog for five minutes. I could hold Brandon's hand for that long. The drugs would kick in soon.

But what if I hadn't given him enough?

What if the pills had lost their potency?

What if he reacted differently than normal people and didn't get sleepy at all?

The hand holding mine relaxed its death grip. That was a good sign.

I yawned. "Hot chocolate is so soothing. Makes me want to curl up and take a nap. How about you? Feeling a little sleepy?"

He shook his head. "No. I'm wide awake." His words came slowly, like Zach's when he's tired but doesn't want to go to bed.

"This sofa is so cushy and soft. Makes me want to sit back and close my eyes for just a minute. Why don't we do that?"

"Whatever my baby wants." He dropped his arm around my shoulders and we settled back on the musty, dusty sofa. His arm got heavier and his breathing slowed.

The doorbell rang.

Brandon sat upright, blinking. Pizza delivery guy had really bad timing.

The doorbell rang again followed by pounding on the door. "Open up! Police!"

"Trent!" I shouted.

"No! He can't have you! You're mine!" Brandon slurred. He stood, swayed, and staggered toward the door. Stumbled. Fell flat on his face.

Finally!

A crash sounded and the door splintered.

I raced across the room, careful not to touch Brandon's motionless body. The hand holding had been quite enough physical contact.

Fred and Trent rushed into the room. Trent held a gun. It was big and black and the most beautiful gun I'd ever seen. I ran to them, tried to fling myself into all four of their arms at once.

"Omigawd, Lindsay!" Trent held my shoulder and examined my face.

"What happened to you?" Fred asked.

I grinned. "You should see the other guy." I stepped back so they could see Brandon.

Chapter Eighteen

"Is he dead?" Trent pressed me tightly against him. I chose to believe it was because he was worried about me, not because he didn't want a murder suspect to escape.

"I don't know. Maybe. I gave him a couple of pills."

"A couple?"

"A few." That was all I was going to admit without talking to my lawyer.

Fred pressed his fingers to Brandon's neck. "He has a pulse. Slow but strong. What kind of pills did you give him?"

"The ones in the bathroom that said they might make him drowsy."

"How many did you give him?" Trent asked.

I watched the slow rise and fall of Brandon's chest and touched my swollen eye, wiggled my loose tooth. I thought of Bob lying dead in the alley, of Ginger with blood in her hair, of Tina's motherless children. "Not enough."

Fred lifted each of Brandon's eyelids and studied his pupils then stood and focused on my face. "Did he do that to you?"

I nodded.

"Trent, you should probably call an ambulance for this guy, but I wouldn't be in any great hurry. I'll get the prescription bottle from the bathroom."

251

He left the room. Trent released me and took out his cell phone.

"Did somebody order a pizza?" From the tentative sound of the boy's voice, I assumed he didn't normally deliver pizzas to homes with the front door broken down.

"Yes," I said. I inhaled the spicy, yeasty smell of the pizza and realized, now that my stomach was no longer clenched into a solid chunk of granite, I was hungry. "Let me get my purse." I took one step toward the coffee table and stopped. My bloody purse still covered my wallet. "Oh." I turned back to Trent. "I...uh...could you pay for the pizza?"

"Sure." He gave me a strange look, took his wallet from his pocket and handed the boy some bills. The boy handed him the pizza and left. "Are you planning to eat this now?"

I stood on one foot then the other. "Yes. No. I was. My purse...Grady Mathis is in the garage. Well, his body is."

Fred strode back into the room with an empty prescription bottle. "This must be what you gave him. He'll sleep for a while, but he's not likely to die." His gaze dropped to the box Trent held. "Is pizza standard for rescue operations?"

Trent handed me the box. "I think we've finally found Grady Mathis."

I pointed Trent to the garage door. Fred followed. Brandon snored.

I set the pizza in the kitchen, walked to the open door and peered into the garage.

Fred stood a couple of feet away from the body, observing, being a law-abiding citizen and not disturbing the crime scene. That probably irritated him to no end.

Trent stood next to the body with his phone pressed to his ear. "I need two ambulances and the crime scene techs. I've got a dead body, an overdose, and a victim who's been beaten."

A victim who's been beaten? A victim? And just when I was ready to forgive him for being a cop.

"You did not just call for an ambulance for me," I said.

"Have you looked at yourself in a mirror lately?"

"I'm fine. I'm not a victim and I'm not going to any stinking hospital."

Fred stepped forward. "In fairness to Lindsay, most hospitals do smell like antiseptic. But you should go anyway. Tina's been asking for you."

"*Tina?* Tina's alive?"

"No thanks to the man asleep in the living room." Trent jerked his head in Brandon's direction. "He followed your car to the park—"

I flinched. "Yeah, he put a tracker on it when I took it to his body shop. He was obsessed with me. When he found Tina sitting in my car, holding the butterfly, he thought she'd stolen them both from me. He thought he killed her."

Trent nodded. "He beat the crap out of her and left her for dead, but she fooled him. Said she'd done it with Ken so many times, she knew how to curl in a ball and protect herself. As soon as he left, she called

911 and when they got there, she demanded to speak to me. She's the reason we found you."

"Brandon told her who he was?"

"No. I took a picture of Grady to the hospital and showed it to her. I knew you were in trouble when a man answered your phone and wouldn't let me speak to you, but I thought it was Grady. That temporary phone didn't have GPS, so we weren't sure where you were. Fred was going to try the shop and I was going to come here. Then I got Tina's call. She recognized Grady's picture but said he wasn't her attacker, that she thought it was the man's son. We came straight here."

"I'm so glad she's okay. I thought he killed her. What about the kids? Are they all right?" I felt certain they were. It would take more than a psycho killer to take those kids down. "Does Ken have them?"

Trent shook his head. "She won't tell us where her boys are. Says they're safe and Ken's not going to get them. He's been at the hospital, making a scene, demanding to see her and demanding to have his kids."

I had a horrible feeling I knew where those kids were. My house was easy walking distance from that park. Running distance for three hyperactive boys. "I've got to get home. By the way, Brandon killed Ginger and Bob and tried to kill Rick."

I started back into the house but Trent grabbed my shoulder. "You can't go anywhere. You're a witness to..." He waved a hand toward my face. "Whatever Brandon did to you. What you did to him.

And you can't drop a bomb like accusing Brandon of killing two people and trying to kill another then just walk out."

I sighed and gave up. Not because Trent told me I couldn't leave but because I didn't have my car. "Can I eat the pizza, or is that evidence too?"

Trent lifted his hands in resignation. "Go ahead and eat the pizza. Just don't disturb anything."

I heard sirens in the distance.

"I need to go somewhere." Fred brushed past me, heading for the front door.

Of course he was leaving. Authorities were on their way. He wouldn't want to be seen by the cops. They might recognize him from the *Most Wanted* posters. Or his presence might compromise his black ops mission. "Aren't you going to stop him from leaving?" I demanded.

"No. He doesn't have to be here."

"You know, don't you?" They'd spent the day together, done all that male bonding, and now Trent knew who Fred really was and I didn't.

Trent frowned. "I know what? You really do need to go to the hospital and let the doctors check you for a concussion. You can come to the station tomorrow and give your statement."

I opened the pizza box and lifted out a piece. The sirens were getting closer. I'd better eat fast. Hospital food is awful, and they frown on pizza deliveries.

☜☞

I did not have a concussion, just two black eyes, a split lip and that loose tooth which the doctor said would probably heal on its own if I quit wiggling it.

They wanted to keep me overnight for observation, but after being stalked by Brandon, I'd had enough observation.

When the doctor finished poking and prodding, I escaped and found my way to Tina's room.

She lay in the stark hospital bed with an IV connected to one arm. Bruises covered everything that wasn't covered by the sheet. I suspected there were plenty more beneath the sheet.

She smiled when I walked in. "You look almost as bad as I do."

I sat down in an uncomfortable chair beside her bed. "That getting knocked around isn't as much fun as it sounds."

"Definitely not. I've had my fill of it. When I get out of here, I'm going to take Ken to court and make sure he never hurts me or my kids again."

"Where is he? I heard he was harassing you."

"He was until that neighbor of yours, the one with white hair, took him aside and talked to him. Then he left and hasn't been back."

Maybe Fred hadn't been running from the cops after all. Maybe he'd come to the hospital to do an intervention with Ken. "What did Fred say to him?"

"I have no idea. Ken was sitting in that chair where you're sitting now. The security guards had already warned him if he didn't stop yelling and threatening me, he'd have to leave. So he was sitting there quietly, leaning close, muttering threats, when Fred came in. He grabbed Ken by the back of his T-shirt and pulled him up. Ken's face got red, and he started swinging. Fred grabbed his arms and whispered something in his ear. Ken went white, Fred wrapped his arm around Ken's shoulders, and they left the room. That's the last I saw of either of them."

Another Fred mystery.

The mystery man appeared in the doorway. "I thought you might need a ride home."

"I do, and I also need to know what you said to Ken."

He settled his lanky frame into the chair on the opposite side of Tina's bed. "I told him about the camera I planted in his bedroom. You know how awful it is to feel that somebody's been watching you."

"I do, but you said you couldn't use the video as evidence since it would be invasion of privacy."

"That's true. Ken and I had a long chat and I explained some things to him. He won't be bothering Tina or the kids anymore. He'll sign the divorce papers, pay a decent amount of child support and give her full custody. Are you ready to go home, Lindsay? Paula and Sophie have been worried about you. Sophie's got a bottle of wine chilling and Zach saved you one of the brownies Paula brought home."

"Is my house still standing?"

"One side's on the ground, but the rest is intact."

Tina tried to sit up in bed, a panic-stricken look on her face. "The boys—"

"He's kidding," I assured her.

"I told them to go to…" She looked at Fred.

"He can read minds. He probably already knows the boys are in my house."

257

Fred nodded. "Lindsay needs a new sofa, but the boys are fine. Paula and Sophie are with them, and they have everything under control."

Oh dear. That meant Zach would get another lesson in being wild and Paula would have to give him a gallon of milk to calm him down. Maybe even some Benadryl syrup.

Tina relaxed onto her pillow. "I didn't know what else to do. I couldn't let Ken get them. Thank you for whatever you did to him."

"Threatened him, brainwashed him, hypnotized him, did a Vulcan mind meld on him," I said. "Fred never tortures and tells."

"Hello, Lindsay." Rick's new girlfriend came into the room. This time she wore street clothes—slacks and a silk blouse. Must be off duty.

"Hi, Robin." I introduced everybody. "Did you hear they have the guy who beat up Rick?"

"I did. I was with him when the police came in to talk to him. I also heard about your ordeal. Are you okay?"

"Oh, sure. My friends are planning a welcome home party. Wine and chocolate. I'll soon be good as new."

"Good friends, chocolate and wine. They all have healing properties."

I turned to Fred. It was time for some answers. "Speaking of my friends, Sophie's been at your house a lot here lately."

He nodded. "She has. I guess I might as well tell you."

"Uh, yeah!" I sat forward, anticipating.

"She didn't want anyone to know."

"Why not? You're both adults."

"She was afraid you'd think less of her."

"You cannot be serious."

"You always seem so fearless. She didn't want to admit she's afraid."

Somehow the conversation had gone completely off the tracks. "Afraid?"

"After Jay Jamison broke into her house. I think it's perfectly normal for her to be fearful. I'm teaching her Karate."

"You're...teaching...her...Karate?"

"Yes. What did you think?"

He knew exactly what I'd thought.

"I thought you were teaching her Karate, of course. And you need to teach me too."

"Okay."

"You need to teach me self-defense and Trent needs to get me a gun and teach me to shoot."

"Trent is not going to get you a gun." The man himself stepped into the room. Apparently someone had put up a big neon sign in the hospital lobby, *Party in Room 207.*

I rose and went to him.

He pulled me gently into his arms. "I've still got a lot of paperwork to do. I don't know when I'll be finished, so I don't know when I'll get to your house. I just wanted to be sure you're okay. The doctor said you refused to spend the night here."

"I'll take her home," Fred said.

"I'll go to her house and check on her later," Dr. Robin offered. How on earth did Rick ever catch the interest of this woman?

I tugged on Trent's hand. "I need to talk to you in the hallway."

"Okay." He followed me out.

I waited as a nurse walked past us then I wrapped my arms around his neck and pressed my lips to his ear. "You can't come to my house tonight," I whispered.

"I can and I will."

"No, the kids are there!"

"Tina's kids?"

"Yes. She had to keep them safe from Ken."

"I figured that was where she sent them. But I'm coming anyway. You shouldn't be alone tonight." He held me away from him and looked into my eyes. "I'll sleep on the sofa."

"That's ridiculous. Brandon's in the hospital—"

"With a police officer outside his door."

I nodded. "So I'm not in any danger."

He let out a huge sigh. "You were kidnapped and beaten. Both your eyes are black, your face is swollen, and your lips look like you've had surgery on them. I'd like to be with you tonight and tomorrow because I love you. I thought maybe you'd want me to be there."

"I do. Of course I do. But...on the sofa?"

"I could stay with you for a couple of hours, then go downstairs before the kids wake up."

I smiled. I wasn't about to tell him how early those kids got up. "Deal."

He gave me a light kiss on my swollen lips. "See you sometime tonight." He started down the hall, away from me.

"Trent!" I ran after him.

He stopped and turned back. I threw my arms around him again. "There's something I need to tell you."

"You want me to get a vasectomy?"

I laughed. "Not tonight."

I leaned back in his arms so I could gaze into his eyes. They sparkled with green fire. "I'm talking to Trent, my boyfriend, not Detective Adam Trent, right?"

"We're the same person, you know."

I sighed. "Maybe, but this information is only for boyfriend Trent's ears."

"Go ahead. I won't tell the cop person."

Cop was probably listening anyway. Cops do that.

I leaned close to his ear. "I lo—" I choked, started coughing.

Trent held me at arm's length. "Are you okay?"

"I'm fine." I straightened and faced him squarely. "I love you."

He grinned. "I love you too."

I smiled as much as I could with swollen lips. "I'll always remember this special moment we shared in the hallway of Pleasant Grove General Hospital."

THE END

RECIPES

My thanks to my cousin, Ruth Waller Jones, of Stafford, KS, for sharing her recipes for Chocolate chip pecan pie, Chocolate Nut Cupcakes, Chocolate Marshmallow Pudding and Chocolate Sheet Cake. Ruth is a wonderful relative and a wonderful cook.

CHOCOLATE CHIP PECAN PIE

1 unbaked 9 inch pie shell

4 eggs
1 cup light corn syrup
6 Tbsp. butter, melted
1/2 cup white sugar
1/2 cup brown sugar
1 Tbsp. flour
1 Tbsp. vanilla
1 cup chopped pecans
1 cup semi-sweet chocolate chips

Beat eggs, corn syrup and sugar. Add butter, flour and vanilla and beat until smooth. Stir in nuts and chips. Pour into pie shell and bake at 350 degrees for one hour or until set.

CHOCOLATE MARSHMALLOW PUDDING

1 cup sugar
1-1/2 cups water
12 marshmallows, cut into fourths
1 tsp. baking powder
1/3 cup cocoa
2 Tbsp. butter
1 Tbsp. vanilla
1 cup flour
1/2 tsp. salt
1/2 cup milk
1/2 cup chopped nuts

Cook water and 1/2 cup sugar for five minutes. Pour into medium casserole dish. Top with marshmallows. Cream butter and remaining sugar. Add vanilla and milk. Combine flour, cocoa and baking powder then add to mixture. Stir until blended. Add nuts. Pour mixture over marshmallows. Cover and bake at 350 degrees for 45 minutes.

CHOCOLATE NUT CUPCAKES

4 ounces semi-sweet chocolate
1 cup butter
1-1/2 cups chopped pecans
4 eggs
1 Tbsp. vanilla
1 cup flour
1-1/2 cups sugar

Melt chocolate and butter. Stir in pecans. Add eggs and vanilla and mix well.

Combine flour and sugar and add to mixture. Mix well, but do not beat.

Fill muffin cups 1/2 full. Bake at 350 degrees for 25-30 minutes. Makes 24 cupcakes.

Note: Cupcakes are dense and moist, not fluffy. They are very rich and can be enjoyed plain, with ice cream or chocolate cream cheese frosting.

Chocolate Cream Cheese Frosting

1 8-ounce pkg. cream cheese
1/2 cup butter, softened to room temperature
1/2 cup cocoa powder
1 Tbsp. vanilla
4 cups powdered sugar

Beat cream cheese and butter. Combine powdered sugar and cocoa. Add to cream cheese mixture. Beat a lot. Add vanilla and beat some more until frosting is of desired consistency.

CHOCOLATE SHEET CAKE

1/2 cup butter
1/2 cup cocoa
1 cup water
1/2 cup oil
2 cups flour
2 cups sugar
1 tsp. soda
1 tsp. salt
1 Tbsp. vanilla
2 eggs, beaten
1/2 buttermilk

Preheat oven to 400 degrees. Grease sheet cake pan and dust with cocoa.

In saucepan bring butter, cocoa and water to a boil. Pour into large mixing bowl and add remaining ingredients. Mix well. Pour into pan and bake for 15-17 minutes. Frost while hot.

Frosting for Chocolate Sheet Cake

1/2 butter
1/3 cup cocoa
1/3 cup buttermilk
1 pound powdered sugar
1 Tbsp. vanilla
3/4 cup chopped nuts

Bring butter, cocoa and buttermilk to a boil. Add powdered sugar and vanilla and beat until spreadable. Add nuts and spread on hot cake.

GOOEY PEANUT BUTTER BARS

1 chocolate cake mix
1 egg
1/2 cup butter, softened to room temperature
1 tsp. vanilla
16 Reese Peanut Butter Cups, unwrapped and frozen
1/2 can sweetened condensed milk
1/2 cup Reese's Pieces

Grease 8 inch square cake pan. Dust with cocoa.

Combine cake mix, egg, butter and vanilla. Beat until a soft dough forms. Press half the dough into baking pan. Arrange frozen Peanut Butter Cups over the top. Press the rest of the dough over the tops of the Peanut Butter Cups. Drizzle half the can of sweetened condensed milk over dough. Sprinkle with Reese's Pieces. Bake at 350 degrees for 30-35 minutes.

About the Author:

I grew up in a small rural town in southeastern Oklahoma where our favorite entertainment on summer evenings was to sit outside under the stars and tell stories. When I went to bed at night, instead of a lullaby, I got a story. That could be due to the fact that everybody in my family has a singing voice like a bullfrog with laryngitis, but they sure could tell stories—ghost stories, funny stories, happy stories, scary stories.

For as long as I can remember I've been a storyteller. Thank goodness for computers so I can write down my stories. It's hard to make listeners sit still for the length of a book! Like my family's tales, my stories are funny, scary, dramatic, romantic, paranormal, magic.

Besides writing, my interests are reading, eating chocolate and riding my Harley.

Contact information is available on my website. I love to talk to readers! And writers. And riders. And computer programmers. Okay, I just plain love to talk!

http://www.sallyberneathy.com

Made in the USA
Columbia, SC
21 August 2023